an
uncomplicated
man

Originally a city girl, Colette has made her home in one of the many former mining villages in County Durham. When not working as a retail manager for a large children's charity she will more than likely be writing, even if it's only a shopping list. She also enjoys cooking, gardening and taking the dog on long walks in the countryside near her home. She has been married for almost forty years and has two grown up sons.

You can keep in touch with Colette via @colettemcauthor on Twitter.

Also by Colette McCormick:

Things I Should Have Said and Done
Ribbons in Her Hair
Not My Brother's Keeper

an uncomplicated man

COLETTE McCORMICK

ACCENT

First published in Great Britain in 2019 by
HEADLINE ACCENT
An imprint of HEADLINE PUBLISHING GROUP

1

Cataloguing in Publication Data is available from the British Library

ISBN 978 1 7861 5 6877

Printed and bound in Great Britain by Clays Ltd, Elcograf S.p.A.

MIX
Paper from
responsible sources
FSC® C104740

Headline's policy is to use papers that are natural, renewable and recyclable
products and made from wood grown in well-managed forests and other
controlled sources. The logging and manufacturing processes are expected
to conform to the environmental regulations of the country of origin.

HEADLINE PUBLISHING GROUP
An Hachette UK Company
Carmelite House
50 Victoria Embankment
London EC4Y 0DZ

www.headline.co.uk
www.hachette.co.uk

For John, John and Andrew
who are my men

DEARDON
July 1957

Alright, I want you to take your time, and in your own words tell me exactly what happened.

DANIEL

Can we just get one thing straight before we go any further? My name is Daniel. It's not Dan and it's definitely not Danny. It's Daniel, Daniel Matthew Laither. Are we clear about that? My name is Daniel.

You might not think it's a big deal, and maybe it's not to some people, but it is to me. It was a big deal to my mum too. Mum said my name was Daniel.

She'd been pregnant with me when my dad went off to war at the end of 1914. He never came back; in fact he was dead before I was even born so it was just the two of us after that. My dad had been a Danny and while Mum wanted to name what would be their only son after him, she was determined that I would always be called Daniel. She said that Danny was the name of the factory worker who buggered off to war and got himself killed the first chance he got, leaving her high and dry with a son to raise.

We didn't have a lot of money, but my mum did her best and she had high expectations for me, her only son. She used to say that with a name like Daniel I would have the chance to do something with my life. She said that I could be better than my father, and for a while I was.

Anyway, she said that I had been christened Daniel so that was my name and I wasn't going to argue with her. No-one argued with my mother, not if they knew what was good for them.

3

My mum had a hard face – it suited her because she was a hard woman. I suppose she had to be, given the shitty hand that life had dealt her. I used to think that if she'd ever been short of food she could have chewed house bricks and not even chipped a tooth. She just had that sort of look about her. None of that mattered to me though, because she was my mum and I loved her.

She had a stand up argument with my dad's mum one day because Gran insisted on calling me Danny.

'His name is Daniel,' Mum said to the woman she used to call 'his mother.' She didn't shout because she didn't have to. In all my life I have never heard my mum shout. She has this way of talking, in a voice that's barely more than a whisper, and she dares you to defy her. That day she spoke slowly and quietly, but it had the same effect as if she was yelling. My Gran was doing all the screaming, not that it did her any good because my mum was adamant. 'His name is Daniel.'

'He should be Danny,' Gran insisted, 'it was good enough for his father.'

Mum pulled herself up to her full height of about four foot eleven and stared at her mother-in-law. 'It might have been good enough for your son,' she said each word slowly and separately, 'but it is not good enough for mine.' Gran opened her mouth to say something but Mum didn't give her the chance, 'and I swear, if I ever hear you call him Danny again, that will be the last time you see him.'

'You can't stop me from seeing him.' Gran laughed as she spoke which didn't help matters.

4

'Just watch me,' Mum replied. She didn't laugh.

Gran always called me Daniel from that day on.

Personally I never wanted to be called Danny. Danny had left me. I know now that it wasn't his fault but when I was a young lad I felt like I was the reason that Dad hadn't come home from the war. I thought that Danny hadn't wanted me enough to come home and if that was the case I didn't want his name.

I got into a fight at school one day with a lad called Chris Metcalfe who kept calling me Danny for no other reason than he knew it would annoy me. He thought he was being clever and he would laugh as he did it, but one day enough was enough and I told him so. I told him if he ever called me Danny again I'd smack him. He did it again two seconds later so I smacked him.

Trouble was I smacked him a bit too hard because I broke his nose. On the plus side, he never called me Danny again. I got the headmaster's cane and my mum's slipper for it, but it had been worth it.

The last time I saw Chris Metcalfe, he called me Mr Laither. He was in my office trying to convince me that he was a good risk to give a mortgage to. He didn't seem to recognise me as the Daniel Laither that he had gone to school with but I would have recognised that crooked nose anywhere.

That's one of the good things about being a bank manager in a small town. Quite often you get to deal with the little shits that made your childhood a misery, but this time you're the one in charge.

Sorry, I don't suppose you care about any of that do you? You want to know about this other business, the one that started with Arthur Braithwaite.

I didn't go to school with Arthur Braithwaite but within half an hour of meeting him I wanted to smack him, too.

Arthur Braithwaite opened his first factory in about 1921. Nobody really knows where his money came from but rumours are that he had something over Charles Matthews who had been his old boss. People said that he knew something about Charles that Charles didn't want becoming public knowledge. Something that Charles was more than willing to pay for as long as Arthur kept quiet.

Just rumours of course, but you know what they say about no smoke without fire.

In the four decades since then Arthur Braithwaite has opened another two factories in town, and is now the single highest employer in the county. The whole town depends on his factories one way or another for its livelihood. If you don't work for him directly, chances are that someone in your family does. Even before this I depended on him for my living. Not directly of course but through our customers. We rely on them having money in our bank and they get their money from him one way or another. I don't have to tell you that he is *the* man around these parts, and that's why I was helpless. We were all helpless when it came to dealing with Arthur Braithwaite.

I first met Arthur Braithwaite last November.

Actually, it goes back a bit further than that.

I was wrong when I said that this business started with Arthur Braithwaite, it really started with William Morris.

I was in my office one day in the middle of November last year when my phone rang and Mrs Warren said, 'I have Mr Morris on the line for you, Mr Laither.' I ran the name through my head, trying to remember who Mr Morris was. I couldn't think of any of our clients with that name. Eventually she prompted me, 'From Head Office.'

'Oh.' It just sort of popped out.

'Shall I put him through?' she asked. It was just a formality because there was no way that I could refuse to take a call from Mr Morris from Head Office, though for the life of me I had no idea what he would want with me. I was surprised that he even knew that I existed. Of course I'd heard of him, but I'd never had a conversation with him before.

I told Mrs Warren to put him through and coughed to clear my throat.

'Danny,' he said, 'Bill Morris here.' There was something about his voice that made me uneasy and it wasn't just the fact that he had called me Danny. I was in two minds about correcting him but didn't get the chance because before I could say anything he was telling me: 'I need a favour, Danny.' That set alarm bells ringing in my head for a start. It couldn't be a good thing for a member of the board to ask you for a favour. They didn't deal with branch managers, not directly anyway.

'Of course Mr Morris,' I said nervously.

'It's not a big thing, Danny,' I opened my mouth with the intention of telling him my name was Daniel but nothing came out. 'I need you to take a meeting.' he said. He'd lowered his voice to little more than a whisper and I imagined him looking over his shoulder as he spoke.

'Of course,' I said, though the thought of it gave me a sick feeling in the pit of my stomach. I couldn't see any situation where he would need to ask me to take a meeting rather than just tell Mrs Warren to schedule it into my diary.

So you see, on reflection, it all started with that phone call from William Morris. If I'd never spoken to him that day none of this would have happened.

It turned out that what he wanted from me was that I take a meeting with a friend of his. It seemed like a straight forward enough request, though I was curious why he had chosen to come to me. I was manager of the smallest branch in town, which made me the manager of the smallest branch in the company.. I was insignificant and I couldn't understand why he hadn't gone to one of the larger branches. It didn't make any sense.

At that point I didn't know who his friend was. All he had told me was that he would treat it as a personal favour if I would take the meeting. He said his friend was a 'local business man who is looking for a line of credit to finance an investment.'

During the conversation that followed it became clear that William Morris wasn't really asking me for a favour at all. He was telling me what to do – which was fair enough,

I suppose, given our relative positions within the bank. I just didn't understand the way he was going about things.

He didn't use the word 'expect' but he might as well have done because he expected me to meet his friend and, what's more, he expected me to give his friend whatever he wanted.

'I'm not going to tell you where to set your rate Danny,' he said, though it was obvious he was, 'but if it were me, I'd be thinking about maybe half a percent less than what we give to the average customer.' I wasn't sure I'd heard him right but before I had the chance to check he was speaking again. 'You won't regret doing business with this man,' William Morris let out a forced, false-sounding laugh. 'Do you know what, Danny?'

'It's…' I started to say but the words wouldn't come out.

'Sorry? What was that?' he said quickly like I had interrupted his speech. I made the excuse that I'd sneezed rather than admit that I'd tried and failed to correct him. 'Oh, bless you,' he said, and I thanked him. 'Anyway, Danny, as I was about to say,' he paused for effect, 'there'll be an opening in the High Street branch in the next year or so and I think that would be right up your street. I think a man like you could do very well in our flag ship branch.' He let that hang in the air for a second or two. 'So, can I tell Arthur's secretary to make an appointment?'

'Arthur?'

'Arthur Braithwaite, have you heard of him?'

Heard of him? Who hadn't heard of him?

He called me Danny three more times before we actually said our goodbyes, the final time being when he said, 'I really appreciate this Danny and...' he paused before adding, '...I'm sure that I can rely on your discretion.'

Through clenched teeth I assured him that he could.

I was as annoyed with myself as I was with him.

I took a deep breath and called Mrs Warren into my office. I told her to expect a call from Arthur Braithwaite's secretary with a view to scheduling a meeting. She mouthed the name but didn't say it out loud. She was barely out of the door before the phone on her desk started ringing and, as I heard her talking, I sat back in my chair and wondered what on earth had happened in the last ten minutes.

I couldn't see how William Morris could ever be friends with a man like Arthur Braithwaite. How would they even know each other? William Morris was the product of a private education and university, whereas it was well reported that Arthur Braithwaite left school when he was twelve years old and had worked his way up from the gutter. Yet Mr Morris had described him as a friend. And then it hit me. It was obvious, really.

There were only two ways that I could see. Either they both belonged to that funny handshake brigade and the boys were looking out for each other, or William Morris was in some way indebted to his 'friend.' There'd been a rumour that Arthur Braithwaite ran a money lending service alongside his more legitimate businesses and I

10

wondered if that could be their connection. I thought that my first idea was more likely, but who knows? I've never got to the bottom of that one.

Mrs Warren came into my office a few minutes later and told me that I would be meeting Arthur Braithwaite in his office the afternoon after next.

You should see Arthur Braithwaite's office. It's got 'I'm a rich bastard' written all over it and right in the centre of it is this big solid oak desk. There's nothing on it apart from a perfectly clean leather-edged blotter and a fountain pen sitting upright in a stand. All show. At least I'd been able to spread my papers out, not that I'd needed them because I might as well have just taken the contract with me. The deal had never been in any doubt. I'd done as Mr Morris suggested and offered an interest rate half a percent lower than our normal rate and there had been no quibbling. No need for negotiation. This deal had already been done between Braithwaite and Morris and I was just the piggy in the middle.

Arthur looked every inch the successful business man too, in his flash suit and golf club tie. He was a man in control of his life and he grinned from ear to ear as he signed on the dotted line. Why wouldn't he? He was borrowing money, a *lot* of money, at practically no interest. I had to force the smile onto my face as he said, 'Pleasure doing business with you, Danny.'

I'd told him my name was Daniel. I had been very specific about it but he'd insisted on calling me Danny all the way through the meeting. 'Maybe we could do this Danny; perhaps could you get me that Danny.' Every time he said anything he called me by name, except it wasn't my name. He made it sound like he was suggesting things, but the tone of his voice made it clear that they were expectations and the fact that he called me Danny was his way of putting me in my place. He knew that he was in charge of what was happening and I could see that he was taking delight in calling me 'Danny' just because he'd worked out that I didn't like it. In lots of ways he reminded me of Chris Metcalfe but this time my hands were tied. I didn't think breaking his nose was a very good idea.

It irritated the life out of me that he called me Danny, I'm not going to deny it, but to be honest he could have called me d'Artagnan if he liked just so long as he signed on the dotted line. I didn't much like the idea of getting on his wrong side. Plus, his mate 'Bill' had made it clear that I had to make sure I gave his friend a deal he could work with. And while he may have implied that the chair behind the desk at the High Street branch would be mine if I played my cards right the flip side of that was that if I failed I'd be out on the street.

After he'd signed the contract he carefully replaced the top on his pen and put it back on its stand. The deal was done. He held his hand across the desk and I took it. However, instead of the gentlemanly handshake that normal people have on these occasions I had to endure my hand being crushed. His hand was as flabby as the rest of him, but Arthur Braithwaite's grip was vice-like and he smiled as I squirmed.

'Let's have a drink to celebrate,' he said after he'd dropped my hand. He reached down and fished two crystal tumblers and a half empty bottle of whiskey from one of the lower drawers of his desk. He poured two healthy measures and handed one of the glasses to me. The blood had still not returned to my fingers and I had to be careful not to drop it.

'You drive a hard bargain, Danny,' he said lifting his glass in a salute, and I couldn't help feeling that he was laughing at me.

I think I forced a smile onto my face but I didn't feel like it. I felt humiliated.

I'd not had any lunch and the whiskey on my empty stomach left me a bit woolly headed. I tried not to let it show. You've got to have a good poker face in my line of work; you can't let the other person know what you're thinking. When there's a man sitting in your office applying for a mortgage or asking for an extension on a loan that he can't pay, you can't let him know the decision too early. You have to be in control.

That's how it is normally anyway, but that day was different.

I wasn't stupid enough to think I was in charge of that meeting and I'd realised that long before I ever walked into his office. It might have looked like I had the upper hand because, technically, I'd arranged the loan on paper, but in this case Braithwaite was the one in charge and I was under no illusion about that. I let it wash over me though because that's how these big businessmen like to behave – you know, the big I am and all that. I'd seen it all before and I was seeing it then.

He glanced at his watch before emptying his glass in two gulps and pushing it away indicating that, as far as he was concerned, the meeting was over. I drained my own glass much quicker than I would do normally, but it was either that or leave some, and it was too good to waste.

The whiskey was still stinging the back of my throat as he offered me his hand once again. I had no option but to take it even though I knew what was coming. His hand was twice the size of mine to start with and once again he squeezed rather than shook.

Luckily for me, the door opened and he immediately let go and walked around his desk to greet whoever had come in. I took the opportunity to shake my wrist and get a bit of blood circulating again.

I heard him say, 'This is a lovely surprise,' and I turned to see that Arthur was hugging a young woman. Well to be honest, when I first saw her all I could see was a shock of blonde hair and a dress but there was something about her that suggested youth and I wasn't wrong.

When he let her go I could see that she was in her early twenties.

'I hope you don't mind Daddy,' she said, using her thumb to wipe away the imprint that her lipstick had left on her father's cheek. 'I was in the area and I thought I'd pop in.' She seemed surprised when she saw me out of the

14

corner of her eye. 'Oh I'm sorry,' she said, 'I didn't realise that you were in a meeting.'

He glanced at me with a smug look on his face. 'Oh we were just about finished, weren't we Danny?' He didn't wait for an answer and with his hand on the base of his daughter's spine he directed her towards me. 'Lucy, let me introduce you to Dan…'

'Daniel,' I said as I offered my hand, 'Daniel Laither.'

She took my hand and, unlike her father's, hers felt like I was holding a feather. 'Hello Daniel,' she said. There was a raspy, almost breathless quality to her voice that was captivating. 'I'm Lucy and I'm very pleased to meet you.'

'Likewise' I could hear a tremor in my voice as I spoke.

So this was Lucy Braithwaite, the golden child that was kept under wraps. When her parents featured in the newspaper attending gala dinners and charity affairs she was never anywhere to be seen. I read somewhere that there had been a kidnap attempt once when she was young, and since then she'd been kept out of the limelight. You just had to see the way that he looked at her to know how precious she was to him, and woe betides anyone who hurt her.

LUCY

I don't know what this has to do with anything but if you want me to tell you about me and Daniel I'll do that and let you be the judge.

I don't remember the exact day that I met Daniel but I know I'd been shopping in the morning with my friend Josie. We'd stopped for a bite to eat at that little café on Bramwell Street, the one with those lovely net curtains covering the windows and where the waitresses wear white aprons. I probably had soup because that's my favourite thing on their menu, but I don't suppose that matters.

We'd looked in a couple of other shops after lunch but when it got to about ten to three I told Josie that I had to go. You see, my father had asked me to meet him at his office at three and I didn't want to be late. At that stage I wasn't sure why he had asked me to meet him, but if there's one thing I've learned, it's to do as my father says.

My father is a wonderful man, and you mustn't listen to the rumours that I'm sure you've heard. I know that he has a bit of a temper but he is kind and generous and he loves me very much. I'm not sure he loves my mother anymore, or even if he ever really did, but he loves me so that makes him a good person in my eyes.

I'd do anything for my father so when he told me to be at his office at three, I didn't think twice.

According to my watch it was one minute to three when I walked through the reception area outside my father's office. He keeps his office in town rather than in one of his factories, but I'm sure you knew that already. Alice Monroe, his secretary, a peroxide blonde with big breasts, was away from her desk when I arrived but she must have caught sight of me as I walked through because she came running after me.

I heard her say. 'Your father's in a meeting, Miss Braith…' but she never got any further than that because I'd already opened the door. My father had told me to go straight in when I got there, he had been very specific about that, so I had no idea why Miss Monroe was making such a fuss. Either he had forgotten to mention to her that I would be coming or she was just trying to look important.

When I opened the door I saw that my father had a visitor. At first I assumed that he must have thought the meeting would be over by three but it had gone on slightly longer than expected. It looked like they were just about finished because my father was already out of his chair and shaking hands with the man. When he saw me he dropped the man's hand and came around his desk. He said something about it being a surprise which was my cue to say that I was in the area and just popped in on the off chance. I now understood why my father had told me to be at his office at three o'clock. He clearly wanted me to meet the man he was with. It wasn't the first time that this had happened and I knew what to do.

17

As he hugged me I saw that the other man was shaking his hand out and bending his fingers like a claw. I had a little laugh to myself because I knew what that meant. It meant that my father had been doing that handshake thing again, the one where he presses really hard like he wants to see if he can make the other man's eyeballs pop out.

The man wasn't looking at us, though; he was more interested in his hand, so I gave my father an extra long hug to give him time to recover.

My father said something about them being finished, put his arm around me and moved me towards the other man. It was obvious that he wanted to introduce me. He does that a lot too.

'Let me introduce...' he said, but didn't get the chance to say a name.

'Daniel,' the other man said as he offered me his hand, 'Daniel Laither.' I held out my hand with the intention of shaking his gently but the man took my hand firmly, looked into my eyes and smiled. Obviously I smiled back, just the way that my mother had taught me because I knew that was what was expected of me when I was introduced to one of my father's business associates. 'Show them plenty of teeth,' she once said to me, so I did.

I told him that I was pleased to meet him and he said the same. His voice shook as he spoke and I thought that he was very sweet. He looked just like a puppy that we'd had when I was a little girl. And you know the good thing about puppies, don't you? They give you unconditional love. All they want to do is please you.

18

I shouldn't laugh but he was practically panting as he looked at me. That happens a lot and I've got to be honest I do like the effect that I have on men. I'm sorry, I don't mean to sound big headed but it's just the way it is. I know I look good and when you add to that the fact that my father is Arthur Braithwaite, there aren't many men that I can't have eating out of my hand.

And those glasses of his, with their black frames and thick lenses just made his eyes seem even bigger. They also made him look intelligent which I thought he must be because my father doesn't have time for idiots.

I noticed that his eyes were blue and they seemed to smile as he looked at me.

I saw my father's face out of the corner of my eye and he was smiling. He was pleased with me.

At that time I didn't know how old Daniel was, but my guess was about forty which turned out to be almost exactly right. I thought that for his age he was very good looking. He was wearing cologne too. I like a man that wears cologne.

Eventually I blinked which broke the spell he was under. He coughed, which I thought was adorable. 'I'll not take up any more of your time, Mr Braithwaite,' he said picking up his battered brown leather briefcase, 'I have everything I need.'

He nodded to my father and smiled at me and said, 'It was a pleasure meeting you Miss Braithwaite.'

'You too, Daniel,' I smiled at him again, 'but please, call me Lucy.'

I watched him leave and after the door had closed behind him I sat in the chair that he had sat in. It was still warm. 'Who's that?' I asked.

'Danny? He's just a bank manager.'

'What happened to Mr Douglas?' I asked. I'd known Mr Douglas from the bank all my life and I was suddenly afraid that something had happened to him. I know he must be getting on bit so I thought he might have died. When I was a little girl he used to give me sweets, though God knows where he got them from. The black market probably. It's only looking back now that I ask myself that sort of question, because we never went without anything during the war. Rationing didn't mean anything to us. I didn't realise that some children never had a toffee for years.

I was relieved when my father said, 'Nothing's wrong with him, I'm just doing some business with a different bank, that's all. It doesn't do to put all your eggs in one basket.'

At the time I thought that was a bit odd because he had dealt with the same bank for as long as I could remember, but I don't really understand business stuff so I didn't say anything. The last thing I wanted to do was appear stupid, especially in front of my father.

My father rang through to ask Miss Monroe to bring me a cup of tea while I waited for him to finish off what he was doing. As she put the cup and saucer on the desk she glowered at me from underneath her long eyelashes but I pretended not to notice. I don't know who she thinks she is... well, I *do* know who she thinks she is... she's my

20

father's mistress, but I'm still his daughter and she ought to show me some respect.

Anyway I don't care about her and her airs and graces, she's just the latest in a long line of tarts my father has slept with. My mother knows about them I'm sure, but what can she do? Nothing. She can't do a thing because my father is a rich, important business man and she is nothing without him. She's pathetic, and from being a little girl I was determined that I would never be like her.

Anyway, to get back to Daniel. My father had called him Danny but he had introduced himself as Daniel and I wondered which he preferred, I would have to ask him next time we met.

And we would meet again. I would make sure of it.

I wondered if he would feed me sweets like Mr Douglas had.

DANIEL

'How did the meeting with Mr Braithwaite go?' I was barely through the door to my office before Bridge followed me in asking the question.

'Fine,' I said as I sat down and started to get the paperwork out of my briefcase.

'No... issues?' he left a suggestive pause between his words. He does that a lot.

'No, no, it was fine,' I said. 'I'm just going to go through everything and then I'll get Johnson to process it.' I was about to ring through to Mrs Warren's desk to ask her if there was any chance of a cup of tea when she appeared with one in her hand. 'You're a mind reader Mrs W,' I said.

'And don't you forget it so just be careful what you think about,' she said with a smile.

I could see Bridge's face pinch up at Mrs Warren's response. He's not one for informality in the work place is our Mr Bridge.

I smiled at her as she put the cup and saucer on the desk in front of me. Ida Warren was a Godsend and we'd worked together for a long time so we got on well enough for her to talk to me like that.

I had a drink of tea while I waited for what I knew was coming next. I didn't have to wait long.

'Well?' she sat herself down in the chair on the other side of the desk.

'Well what Mrs Warren?' I struggled to keep a straight face.

She sighed heavily, dropped her head to the right and pursed her lips. 'You know fine well what I'm asking you Daniel Laither,' she said.

'Mr L…' Bridge started to say something but we both held a hand up to silence him.

'What's he like?' she whispered as she leaned forward in the chair.

There was no point asking who she meant because we all knew.

'You know Mr Laither can't discuss private matters.' Bridge said.

She swivelled in her chair, and looked him squarely in the eyes. Anthony Bridge might intimidate some of the younger members of staff but it didn't work with her. 'For your information Mr Bridge,' she emphasised his name, 'As Mr Laither's personal secretary, I am fully aware of what you refer to as 'private matters.' I see all of his mail, I type all of his letters, and I make all of his appointments.' Bridge looked away at something on the wall and Mrs Warren turned back to face me. I had to bite my lip to stop myself from smiling. I might have enjoyed her taking my Assistant Manager down a peg or two but I didn't have to show it.

'Am I going to have to ask you again?' it sounded like she was chastising a child.

'What would you like to know, Mrs Warren?' I enjoyed teasing her.

She wanted to know if he was as handsome as he looked in the newspapers and I had to tell her that I really didn't feel qualified to answer that one. She wanted to know what his suit was like. 'I'll bet it was smart,' she said and I had to admit that it was. 'Aye, he'll not get his from John Collier's,' she said and I assured her that that appeared to be the case.

'I'll be going then sir if there's nothing else,' Bridge was at the door.

'Thank you Mr Bridge,' I said, 'I'll see you later for a catch up, shall we say four-thirty' He nodded his head and left.

As I finished my tea I answered Mrs Warren's questions. She wanted to know what Arthur Braithwaite's office was like, how his secretary dressed and what brand of typewriter she used.

The answer to the first bit was easy. His office was over the top grand. All wood panelling and thick carpet. As well as the oak desk with the clean blotter and the fountain pen, I told her about the wall that was shelved top to bottom and filled with books that had probably never been read.

'Are you sure they were real books?' she asked and I said I didn't think so. Then I told her about the wall that was covered with pictures of him and his wife with famous people and finally I told her about the window that took up one whole wall. 'Flashy then?' she said as she grabbed the saucer that my now empty cup was sitting on.

I nodded and we laughed.

It seemed she had forgotten about the secretary and her typewriter.

At four-thirty on the dot, there was a knock on my door. Mr Bridge is nothing if not punctual. Not a minute to or a minute past. I suppose you could call him a stickler.

'Come in Mr Bridge,' I called and he did. He sat in the chair opposite me.

'You wanted to see me.'

'Just to go over the details,' I pushed three sheets of paper towards him. He took his glasses from his inside pocket and started to read. It was a pretty standard contract, the same clauses and appendices as all of our loan contracts. The only difference was…

'The interest rate?' he looked at me, then back to the paper in his hand before looking at me again. 'The interest rate,' he said again but it was a statement this time and not a question, 'it's not right.'

'Yes it is.'

'But it's half a percent lower than our standard rate.'

I tried to come up with a way of justifying it that didn't involve William Morris.

'Mr Braithwaite has taken out a substantial loan with us,' I explained, 'and even at this rate, the bank will still make a healthy profit.'

He raised an eyebrow. 'And the board agreed?'

'Yes,' it wasn't really a lie as one of the senior board members had suggested it.

He stared at the sheet of paper in his hand. Occasionally he looked up but most of the time his eyes were down and moving over the words and figures.

'One thing I don't understand though Daniel,' he said eventually.

'What's that Anthony?' we dispensed with formality when it was just the two of us.

'Why us? Why come here? Why not the main branch on the High Street?'

I had asked myself the same question.

I told Isobel about Arthur Braithwaite that evening as we ate dinner. I didn't mention him by name, I would never do that, not even to my wife, but I told her that I had had a meeting with a new client, an important one, one that would hopefully get me noticed at Head Office.

'This could be the start of something,' I told her, 'if I get moved to the High Street Branch there'll be a pay rise. You might even get your semi on Chestnut Avenue.'

Her eyes lit up at that prospect but as always she was cautious. 'Best not count any chickens just yet,' she said, but I could tell from the look in her eyes that she was already picking out the type of curtains she wanted for the bay windows. Isobel didn't ask for much out of life, she wasn't a social climber like the wives of some of my colleagues, but when she dreamt it was of the semi-detached houses on Chestnut Avenue.

Later, after we'd eaten our food and the dishes were washed and stacked back in the cupboard, we sat in matching armchairs at either side of the fire place. Isobel sewed buttons onto shirts and I read the paper.

I flicked the page over and there he was. Arthur Braithwaite was in full evening dress with his wife on his arm, smiling for the camera as they arrived at a charity function. His daughter was nowhere to be seen.

I really didn't like the man. Mrs Warren had been right when she called him flashy. Everything about him said 'look at me, look what this lad from the gutter has done.' And everything about him, from his made-to-measure suit to his office with its oak desk and photographs of famous people, was there to show just what an important man he was. Like anyone needed reminding, the newspapers told us all often enough. It was just like his refusal to call me Daniel and the bone crushing handshake, both were designed to show me that he was in charge.

What an idiot.

Nice daughter though, very pretty.

The following afternoon I was in my office trying and failing to come up with a way that we wouldn't have to foreclose on a mortgage held by a young man and his wife with a baby on the way when there was a tap on my door. I looked up to see that Johnson, the senior clerk had popped his head into the room.

'I'm sorry to bother you sir,' he said, 'but there's someone to see you.'

'Who is it?' A glance at my diary which lay open on my desk confirmed that I wasn't expecting anyone.

'It's M...'

'Me,' she walked around Johnson and into the room.

'Miss Braithwaite.' She was the last person that I expected to see. Her father maybe; but not her. I pushed my chair back and stood up.

'Daniel,' she elongated my name and looked at me with her head leaning to one side and her hands on her hips. 'What did I tell you yesterday? Call me Lucy.'

'Of course,' I coughed to cover my embarrassment and moved swiftly around the desk to pull the chair out for her. 'What can I do for you... Lucy?' I had to force myself to be so informal.

She smiled at me as she sat down.

'Could I get a cup of tea please?' She directed her question at Johnson who was still hovering by the door. 'Weak, lots of milk.' Johnson looked at me briefly before backing out of the room. He closed the door quietly.

Lucy crossed her legs and her skirt rode up just enough to show her knee. She giggled as I looked away quickly. I could feel the warmth of a blush rising up my neck and onto my face. I hadn't blushed in years and I felt uncomfortable doing it now. I silently thanked God when there was another knock at the door.

'Yes,' I noticed that my voice was an octave or two higher than it normally was and I coughed again.

Mrs Warren came in balancing two cups and saucers on a tray. She put a cup of tea down in front of Lucy and the other in front of me. She kept her eyes down and left as quickly as she could.

My legs started to tremble and I realised I was still standing up, stunned by her, like an idiot. I didn't understand what was happening. I was a grown man not a school boy for God's sake.

'Lovely,' Lucy said uncrossing her legs and moving to the edge of her seat. She used both hands to lift her cup to her lips and looked at me provocatively over the rim. She left a hint of her lipstick on the cup as she took a sip. She replaced it in its saucer and settled back in the chair once again with her hands joined together in her lap.

'So... Danny...' her eyes sparkled as she spoke, 'you don't mind if I call you Danny, do you?'

I took the opportunity to tell her, 'I'd rather you call me Daniel if you don't mind Miss... Lucy.'

'Daniel it is then.' When she smiled at me it was like there was something happening inside my chest. It felt like my heart was trying to burst its way through my rib-cage. I was over-whelmed by the reaction the mere sight of this girl had caused in me and it took everything I had to maintain my composure.

I'd half expected her to say that her father had sent her, but it soon became clear that she hadn't come on business of any sort. There was no message from her father, no question that needed to be answered. It appeared that Lucy had come to see me just because she had wanted to.

Why would she do that? It didn't make any sense. She was just a girl of... what, twenty-two... twenty three... and I was a middle aged man. We had absolutely nothing in

29

common and surely she had something better to do on a Thursday afternoon.

I glanced at the papers that I'd been looking at before Lucy arrived. I really needed to concentrate on finding a way to help Mr and Mrs Taylor meet their mortgage commitments, but I found that the only thing that I really wanted to give my attention to was the sound of Lucy's voice. That raspy breathlessness of it that I had noticed the day before was just so appealing. She was talking but if I'm honest I don't really know what she was talking about. I was listening to the sound, not the words.

The sound had stopped.

'Are you alright Daniel?' I realised her tone had changed. 'Daniel? Are you alright?' She repeated.

I cleared my throat, 'Yes I'm fine thank you.'

'I'm talking too much aren't I?' She didn't sound like she meant it.

'No, no, of course you're not.' I could listen to her for hours.

'My mother says I do that a lot, you know, talk too much.' She leaned forward, offering me a seductive glimpse of her breasts that were encased in a tight jumper. I felt myself getting warm again. 'But I don't, not really,' she said, 'I only talk a lot to people I find interesting.' She paused, looking deep into my eyes. 'And I find you interesting, Daniel,' another pause, 'very interesting.'

I hadn't meant to giggle, but I did, and when I look back on what happened between us I know that that was the moment I fell under the spell of Lucy Braithwaite. That was the moment that I was lost to her. That was the moment that changed my life.

A few minutes later she announced that she had things to do. 'And you need to get on.' She nodded to the papers that I had quickly stacked together. 'I'm sorry to have taken up so much of your time,' she said as she held her hand out to me.

'Not at all Lucy,' this time her name dropped off my lips easily and naturally.

When we shook hands she held onto mine a fraction longer than was necessary but I didn't object. I was enjoying the way her hand felt in mine. She had soft hands.

She was about to walk through the door when she turned her head and looked at me over her shoulder. 'Bye Daniel,' she breathed, 'See you soon.'

And then she was gone.

I sat in my chair and wondered what the hell had happened during the previous half hour. I stared at the chair she had sat in and wondered if I had imagined it. But no, there was her cup with the remnants of her lipstick around the rim and there was a floral smell lingering in the air. I breathed in deeply and was enjoying the sensation when there was a tap on the door and Mrs Warren came back in.

'Can I take those cups away for you Mr Laither?' she asked, emphasising my name.

'Of course Mrs Warren,' I said.

I could tell that she was itching to ask about my unexpected visitor and I was grateful when she didn't.

'Thank you Mrs Warren,' I said, but I didn't meet her eyes.

LUCY

I was out shopping with my friend Janet that morning, the day after I'd met Daniel in my father's office. Janet was looking for a birthday present for her boyfriend and after she'd bought him a jumper or something we'd had a bite to eat at that little café on Stafford Street, the one that does the lovely scones.

I love to go to cafes, don't you?

Anyway, I knew the bank that Daniel worked at was just a couple of streets away so when I left Janet and, instead of going straight home, I decided to pop in to see if he was about.

I walked through the doors and tried to get my bearings. There was a counter to the right of me with two windows and a desk to the side of that where a man was sitting writing something in a book. He looked up as I walked in. I always wear heels and they were clicking on the wooden floor. He put down his pen and stood up.

'Good afternoon Miss,' he said quietly, 'may I help you?'

'I'm here to see Mr Laither,' I said.

He held up a finger in that 'hold on a moment' way and went back to his desk to consult the other book that was sitting there. He ran his finger down the page and came back looking apologetic.

'Excuse me,' he said, 'but do you have an appointment? As far as I can see Mr Laither isn't expecting anyone this afternoon.'

'He's not expecting me.' I said, 'but he will want to see me.' That's the thing about being Arthur Braithwaite's daughter, you see, I'm used to getting what I want and I don't take no for an answer.

'I'm sorry Miss, but Mr Laither doesn't see anyone without an appointment.'

I was starting to feel sorry for the poor man, he looked so embarrassed. I decided to put him out of his misery. 'Would you please tell Mr Laither that Miss Braithwaite is here to see him?'

That made him change his tune. He nodded his head and asked me to wait where I was. Well I wasn't going to do that, so I let him get a few steps ahead of me and then I followed him. As he tapped on the door that had Daniel's name on it I looked at the desk that sat outside his office. It was clearly Daniel's secretary's desk but thank goodness she wasn't there because if she was anything like Miss Monroe she'd have tried to stop me in my tracks. I wondered if Daniel was sleeping with his secretary too. The name plate on her desk described her as a 'Mrs' but that didn't mean anything.

The man I was following had popped his head around the door he had knocked on and I could hear him mumbling that there was someone here to see him. I had just heard Daniel ask who it was when, out of the corner of my eye I saw the secretary coming along the corridor. That was when I decided to take the bull by the horns and breezed into Daniel's office.

You should have seen his face; he was so surprised to see me.

'Miss Braithwaite,' he said in a terribly formal way as he stood up.

I had to correct him about that. I wanted him to call me Lucy. He seemed a bit uncomfortable saying my name at first but he managed it and it was adorable watching him force himself to be so informal. Bank managers are so stuffy.

I remember asking if I could call him Danny and that was when he said he would prefer it if I call him Daniel. I didn't mind at all. Daniel suited him in a way that Danny never could.

A couple of minutes later Daniel's secretary brought us a cup of tea each and I noticed that she didn't look at me directly which I thought was a bit rude. She probably hated the fact that someone without an appointment had got into the inner sanctum and was kicking herself for not being at her station to protect her boss from young women bursting into his office. I decided that Daniel probably wasn't sleeping with her. Not unless he had a taste for much older women that is.

Anyway, I caught Daniel looking at my legs as I crossed them. He looked away quickly but it was too late, I'd seen him. I had a little giggle to myself and I felt bad about that because I shouldn't have – giggled that is – I'd meant to cross my legs. I'd wanted to see if he would take the bait and he had. I'd wanted to see if he found me attractive and there was no denying his reaction. I know I sound like I'm blowing my own trumpet but I do have really good legs and men often look at them.

I was there for about half an hour and we spent the whole time talking, or rather I did. I like to talk, I like the sound that talking makes. I know that makes me sound mad but it's just the truth and I have promised to tell the truth. Daniel didn't seem to mind me talking, though he did seem to drift off at one point.

As I was leaving he called me Lucy again but this time he said it as easily as he would his own name, and that's when I knew that he was mine for the taking.

36

DANIEL

I thought about Lucy a lot over the next few days, which I know was wrong of me given that she must have been half my age, and I have a wife, but I couldn't help it. I realise how pathetic that makes me sound but it's just the way it was.

One afternoon at the beginning of last December the telephone on my desk rang and I picked it up. I waited for Mrs Warren to speak.

'I have Mr Braithwaite for you sir,' she said.

'Put him through please, Mrs Warren,' I said and I cleared my throat while I waited for the connection to be made. I didn't want my voice giving away just how nervous the man made me feel.

'How are you, Danny boy?' he was as loud and brash as the last time I'd spoken to him.

I felt the back of my neck tingling like the hairs were standing on end. It took everything I've learned during my time at the bank to keep my voice controlled. 'I'm very well thank you Mr Braithwaite, how are you?'

'Never better Danny,' he said, 'never better. I was just ringing to say that the paperwork has arrived.'

I didn't believe that was the reason he'd rang but I went along with him and said, 'I trust everything is in order.'

'I meant it when I said you drive a hard bargain, Danny,' he laughed, 'but there's nothing there that I can't work with.' He was so bloody patronising. I forced a laugh and waited nervously for what might be coming next. I wondered how he was going to belittle me now. Here I was, stuck in the middle of a game he was playing with William Morris and I couldn't see a way out. I felt like that bit of string that a cat plays with; I was totally at his mercy.

'Anyway, Danny,' he said, 'that's not why I'm ringing.' My stomach did somersaults as I waited for what was coming next. It came as a relief when he said, 'I want to set up a lunch date, give me a chance to say thank you.'

I covered the mouthpiece so that he couldn't hear me letting out the breath I'd been holding. I can't say he's a man I would choose to socialise with but what harm could a business lunch do?

I almost told Isobel about it – the lunch that is, not who I'd be eating with. Like I've said, I never discuss my clients with her but I almost told her where I would be having lunch. She would have been so impressed.

Looking back if I'd told her about it, things might not have turned out the way they did. Hindsight is a wonderful thing.

The waiter who had showed me to the table pulled the chair out so that I could sit. Arthur Braithwaite was already there.

Thank God that he didn't try to shake my hand.

'Danny, glad you could make it,' he said. I flicked my eyes to the left and then the right, taking in the unoccupied tables either side of us. The restaurant had appeared busy as I'd walked through it but the section we were in was deserted. 'I appreciate the privacy,' he said and I could have kicked myself for being so obvious. I should have known that it wouldn't go unnoticed. He's the type of man who misses nothing.

A bowl of soup that I hadn't ordered was placed in front of me by a waiter I hadn't realised was there. Another white coated waiter was placing a similar bowl in front of my host while a third one showed him a bottle of wine.

'I'm sure it's excellent as always Martin,' Braithwaite said and then gestured with his hand, 'but please, let Danny Boy be the judge.' Martin gave a reverential nod of the head before offering the bottle to me. I wanted to tell Martin that I didn't know who Danny Boy was but I thought better of it. Instead, like a good boy, I did as I was told and read the label and felt instantly sick though I wasn't sure if that was because of my inability to stand up for myself or what Martin was showing me.

I'm not much of a wine drinker but even I recognised the label on the bottle as the preferred tipple of the rich and famous, and I knew the value of what I would be drinking with my lunch. Martin poured a little into my glass and I could see my hand shaking as I lifted it to my lips. The wine was cold and crisp and as I felt it slip down my throat I thought I could taste something fruity.

I nodded my approval to Martin who made a big show of filling first my glass and then Braithwaite's. He deposited the bottle in a cooler that had appeared by the side of the table before backing away to join the others.

It was just the two of us.

Braithwaite picked up his spoon and scooped up some soup. 'Eat up Danny,' he said. 'I hope you don't mind but I ordered for you. I think you'll like it.'

I wondered if it would make any difference to him if I did object and decided that it probably wouldn't. I picked up my own spoon and started to eat. I couldn't fail to notice the noises that my lunch date made as he ate. A slurping noise accompanied every spoonful of soup, though if he realised he was doing it he didn't appear to care. Men like him don't have to care though do they. Men like him can do what they want and behave however they like. Not for the first time I wondered if I'd done the right thing when I agreed to do business with this man. But what choice had Mr Morris given me? What choice had Mr Morris had?

When the soup was finished the waiters appeared again to remove the plates and two more appeared instantly to place the main course in front of us. Martin appeared to top up our glasses and I wondered exactly how many waiters were hiding in the shadows just to wait on us.

'Lucy tells me she stopped by your office the other day.' Braithwaite said as he popped a piece of pork into his mouth.

'Yes,' I took a sip of wine to moisten my mouth which suddenly felt coated in sand.

'Nice girl?' he made it sound like a question which I wasn't sure how to answer, so I pretended to chew my meat long after it had been swallowed.

Braithwaite's forearms rested on the edge of the table, a piece of cutlery in each hand. 'She is my world,' he said in a gentler voice than I had heard him use before, but it was no less menacing for that. He put more food into his mouth and talked while he ate. 'There's nothing that I wouldn't do for Lucy,' he said, 'nothing that I wouldn't do to make her happy or keep her safe. When she was young it was easy, I could buy her whatever she wanted to make her happy and send her away to boarding school to keep her safe. It broke my heart to see her go but I had to keep her from harm.' Was it uncertainty that I saw in Arthur Braithwaite's eyes? 'I'm sure I don't have to tell you that I have a few enemies,' he laughed out loud. 'That's the trouble when you're a success you see, people get jealous. The thing is Danny, I wasn't born with a silver spoon in my mouth,' even though he was whispering there was something about his voice that made it sound like a shout, 'and everything I've got I've made for myself. I'm not going to say that I didn't make a profit out of the last war, but what can I say? I made the best of a bad job, that's all. And I did my bit for King and country in the first one. I was in the army. I saw action. Did you see action, Danny?' he asked before he put the last of the pork in his mouth.

'No,' I admitted with more than a hint of embarrassment, 'they wouldn't have me… a medical thing.' No-one knew how often I'd thanked the god that gave me flat feet. Every time I'd heard the news from the front I'd sent up a little prayer of gratitude.

'Oh well, can't be helped, not your fault,' he said as he drained his glass. Martin appeared again to refill it. He offered to fill mine but I declined. Like I said, I'm not

41

much of a wine drinker and I was already feeling a bit light headed.

'Anyway, like I was saying, I have enemies and the thing is Danny,' he paused with the wine glass halfway to his mouth, 'I don't like enemies.' His eyes narrowed and the hint of a smile crossed his lips. 'Do you know what I do to my enemies, Danny?' I had put the last of my own food in my mouth and chewed it slowly while I waited for the punch line. 'I crush them,' he said.

I felt slightly uncomfortable as I tried to decipher the message behind the words. What was it he was trying to tell me? 'Don't look so worried, Danny,' Braithwaite laughed, 'I'm just the opposite with my friends. I treat my friends to slap up lunches and fancy wine.'

I guessed that made us friends, but I wasn't sure I was any happier with that prospect.

As our plates were cleared away, the man who had shown me to my seat – and the only member of staff in a black jacket – appeared at Braithwaite's shoulder. He leaned down and whispered something. Braithwaite's face instantly lit up. 'Of course she can, William,' he said, pushing William gently to speed him on his way. He wiped his food-covered mouth with his napkin and dropped it on the floor as he stood up. There was a smile on his face, a real smile this time, not the one that I'd seen before, the one that made me nervous. When I turned to see what had created such a reaction I wasn't surprised to see that it was the only thing that could have.

Lucy was walking towards us with the brighter lights from the front of the restaurant creating a halo effect around her.

I think I was probably smiling myself.

I stood up too but she only had eyes for her father. They embraced and I could see the genuine affection that they shared. Maybe he wasn't all bad, he clearly loved his daughter. But they say that Hitler loved his mother so maybe that wasn't enough to recommend him.

'This is a surprise,' Braithwaite held his daughter at arm's length like he was admiring her as he spoke.

'I hope you don't mind, Daddy,' she said, 'but when I heard that you were meeting Daniel for lunch today I just had to come and see if you were still here.' I wondered if he had noticed what she had called me Daniel, but I doubted that he had or that cared.

'Of course I don't mind, I'm always happy to see you, though is it really me you came to see?' he smiled as they shared a secret look. Martin was already laying more cutlery on the table. 'You know what she wants,' Braithwaite laughed, 'and get one for Danny here, too.'

'Are you not having one Daddy?' Lucy giggled as she spoke.

'No darling, you know it's not really my thing. I'm more of an apple pie and custard man. Anyway, Danny and me had just about finished so I'll leave you two to enjoy your dessert in peace.'

That was the second time she had arrived just as he was finished with me, but at the time it hadn't really seemed suspicious at all.

He gave his daughter another hug and I stood up and offered my hand to him. It was the polite thing to do; I mean he had just bought me the most expensive meal I had ever eaten. Once again I could feel the bones in my hand creaking under his grip and I wondered what the hell was wrong with the man?

'How many times have I told you, Daddy,' Lucy said in a jokey voice, 'it's not Danny its Daniel. He prefers Daniel.'

'Bye Danny,' Arthur said and I couldn't help but feel like I was being laughed at.

I had been sitting opposite her father and now I was sitting next to her, so close that I could smell the floral perfume that she was wearing. It was the same as she had worn that day in my office. It was heady but not overpowering, and I took a deep breath just so that I could get more of the smell in my lungs. She was wearing red lipstick and as she spoke I saw the whiteness of her teeth exaggerated against the redness. Something about her mouth had captivated me and I was reading her lips rather than listening to her voice.

'I'm sorry if I interrupted something really important,' she said.

'Not at all,' I was a little embarrassed when I realised that I was staring at her.

'Were you talking about something really important?' She furrowed her eyebrows which gave her face a serious look.

'No,' I said, allowing myself to relax a little. 'It was more of a thank you lunch than a business meeting.' When I thought about it we hadn't really talked about anything other than how much Arthur Braithwaite loved his daughter and how he would do anything to make her happy. Thinking about it now, there *had* been something serious about that conversation. Serious and some might say sinister.

'I'm so glad that you and Daddy are going to be working together,' she said as she placed her napkin on her lap in eager anticipation of whatever it was that Martin hadn't needed to be told. She flattened the linen onto her lap before she looked at me. 'Some people are a little wary of doing business with my father but you mustn't believe everything that you hear about him or read in the papers. He's a good man, really. I know sometimes he can be a little...' she searched the wall opposite her for the right word, 'unorthodox, but he's not a criminal. He's never broken any law.' I was inclined to think that it might be more a case of never being convicted but I didn't correct her. There was no need to shatter her illusions about what a good man her father was.

'I don't judge anyone,' I said, aware that it sounded a bit *holier than thou*.

Lucy laughed, 'Isn't that your job, Daniel?'

'Only when it comes to their ability to meet the required repayment schedule,' I laughed too.

'Well you have no worries on that score,' she told me and I knew that she was right. I told her I was glad to hear it.

Our desserts arrived. Two waiters to deliver two small plates of food seemed a little unnecessary to me but I guessed this was how the other half lived. I looked at what had been placed in front of me.

'It's crème brûlée,' Lucy told me, 'it's my favourite. Have you ever had it before?'

'No,' I admitted though I didn't tell her that I had never even heard of it. I was more of an apple pie and custard man myself and it scared me that I had something in common with her father.

'I had it in France,' she said as she broke a thin, crisp layer of caramel with the back of her spoon to expose the creamy custard beneath, 'and I just fell in love with it.' She took a spoonful of it in her mouth and I watched her savour its taste. I caught myself wondering if she had that look on her face every time she felt pleasure, but quickly tossed the thought aside as being highly inappropriate.

Oh well, I thought, *first time for everything* and I copied her movements and wouldn't have been surprised if I'd copied her reaction too. It was delicious.

'In this country you used to only be able to get it in London,' I suddenly realised that she was talking and gave her my attention again, 'but Jean Paul the head chef here is from Paris, so naturally he makes it. Don't you just love it?'

'It's very nice.'

'I'll bet you've never had anything like it before, have you Daniel?'

'No,' I said as I scraped up the last spoonful and put it in my mouth, 'and it was quite delicious.'

'How would you like to have something else you've never had before?' Lucy purred, 'something just as delicious as that crème brûlée?'

'What else do you have in mind?' I asked, genuinely wondering what else the Parisian maestro in the kitchen could concoct.

'Me.'

I meant to say no, I meant to tell her I was married, I meant to point out that I was almost twice her age but I didn't. Instead I allowed myself to end up in a hotel room with her.

'Don't look so worried Daniel,' she said as she slinked across the floor towards me, 'You'll enjoy it.' She took off my glasses, carefully folded the arms in and placed them on the bedside table. As she stood in front of me, just inches away from me, I could feel the touch of her breath on my lips. All thoughts of her father, of my wife, or anything else were dismissed as I moved my lips to hers and kissed her. They were soft and warm and I could taste her. She had been right when she had said I would find her delicious.

47

I couldn't help myself. I had tasted her and now I wanted more. Would it sound silly if I said I felt powerful? It was like I was stronger than I had ever been before; she had made me feel stronger because she wanted me. I pulled her towards me, crushing her breasts against my chest. Without realising it I had flicked my tongue into her mouth, which was something that Isobel found repulsive, yet here I was doing it to Lucy and she was responding.

With eager hands we ripped the clothes from our bodies and within minutes we were naked. Moments later I knew just how sweet Lucy really was.

I lay on my back, spent and more satisfied than I had ever felt in my life. I had never imagined that it was possible for a man to feel the way I did at that moment and all of it was down to the woman who nestled against my shoulder with her hand gently stroking the soft down on my chest.

I spared the briefest of moments to think about my wife. Isobel had never made me feel the way that I did then. But did that make this right? No, of course it didn't. Isobel might not have Lucy's youth, or her figure, or her looks, but she was my wife. She had been my wife for fifteen years and she deserved my loyalty. I knew that she would be at home taking care of jobs around the house, maybe preparing something for our tea, and I was disgusted with myself for being where I was. However, I wasn't disgusted enough to do anything about it and I pulled Lucy in closer to me instead.

Lucy took this as a sign of encouragement and lifted herself onto her elbow. She smiled at me, then she kissed me, and before I knew it she was astride me and I was doing something else that I had never done to a woman before.

Later Lucy said 'Thank you,' as she sat on the edge of the bed rolling a stocking up her thigh, 'that was wonderful.' She stood up and straightened her skirt. I remember thinking that I had never seen anything as beautiful in my life, and that made me even more disgusted with myself because I had never looked at Isobel like that, I had never felt that way about her.

Before we left the room we kissed one last time, except that it wasn't really the last time. I knew there would be other times like this and I was grateful for that.

It was after four o'clock when we left the hotel. The receptionist, a tall grey haired man in a dark blue suit, smiled at Lucy as he nodded his head to one side. He eyed me suspiciously.

Two taxis were sitting by the kerb and Lucy opened the door of the first one. Before she got in she turned to me and said. 'Thank you again for a lovely afternoon, Daniel. I hope we can do it again... soon.' She pursed her lips in a kissing motion before climbing into the taxi and giving the driver directions. As the car pulled away she turned in her seat and waved at me. I lifted my hand and waved back.

LUCY

My father and I were having breakfast together when he told me that he was having lunch with Daniel. I think it was the Wednesday of the week after they'd done whatever deal they'd been doing in his office. I don't suppose it really matters what day it was, does it? It was round about then anyway.

He said that he was meeting Daniel at Poplar Lodge at one o'clock and he told me that I should come along about two and meet them there. He said that I'd be just in time for dessert so it would be worth my while. He told me that when I arrived I was to act like I had just decided to pop in. It wasn't to look like we had planned it.

I'll bet you're asking yourself why my father wanted me to do that but it's obvious really. He wanted me to… how can I put this… he wanted me to keep Daniel sweet, use my charms on him. He'd seen as well as I had the way that Daniel had looked at me, and my father wanted to use that to our benefit. When I say 'our,' I mean the company's benefit of course. I didn't know the particulars of what they were doing together but if my father needed me to help him in some way I was more than willing to do it. The business will be mine one day after all.

Anyway, he'd only asked me to arrive at Poplar Lodge in time for dessert so it was no hardship.

Have you ever been to Poplar Lodge? Their food is delicious. My father likes to have his business meetings there because it impresses people and my father likes to impress people. He sometimes takes me when it's just the two of us, but he rarely takes my mother.

Obviously she'd heard us talking about it at breakfast but she waited an hour or so before she asked me about it. She was getting ready to leave the house and tried to make it sound like she didn't really care but I could tell that she did. She hates it when she doesn't know what's going on

'Who's he wining and dining today?' she asked. I told her he was meeting Daniel and she asked who that was.

'He's a bank manager,' I told her.

She was checking her make up in the hallway mirror, using her little finger to tidy the lipstick in the corner of her mouth. 'What happened to Frank Douglas?' she asked, 'did he finally die?'

'No, Daniel doesn't work for that bank, he's the manager of a different one, the one near Daddy's factory.' She pulled a face because she doesn't like me calling him Daddy. And she absolutely hates it if I call her Mummy. I like to do it now and again just to annoy her. Besides, I don't understand what her problem is, they're just names. What would she rather I call them? Ma and Pa?

'Why's your father using a different bank?' she picked up her handbag and a set of keys from the table in the hallway.

'Don't know,' I said, though I wouldn't have told her even if I did.

51

'Oh well, must go, see you later.' She had closed the door before I'd even said goodbye.

I wasn't upset because she's always a bit like that. She doesn't like how close my father and I are. She thinks he has ruined me and I once heard them having an argument in which she called me a spoiled brat. I didn't see it happen but I think he might have hit her for that because she didn't speak to me for a week and wore sunglasses even in the house.

I took a lot of care getting ready that day. My father would expect me to look nice but it had to be casual enough to look like I'd just been out shopping. I couldn't arrive made up to the nines and wearing a posh dress. I didn't just want to look good because it was expected of me, though; I wanted to look good because it's how I like to look. I don't understand how a woman can not care about how she looks.

I took care choosing my clothes and eventually settled on a black pencil skirt and tight red jumper. As I looked in the mirror I was pleased with what I saw.

I got to Poplar Lodge right on time, and my father looked pleased to see me when William took me to their table. I knew straight away that my father had been right to tell me to come because Daniel seemed pleased to see me too. I don't know if he realised he was doing it but he smiled, not in that polite way that people do when they think that they have to smile, but in the honest way when you know it's what they are feeling.

My father had said I was to keep Daniel sweet but he hadn't told me how to do it. I had my own plans and I could tell that he would be putty in my hands.

My father left shortly after I got there saying something about dessert not really being his thing. It is – you just have to look at him to know he likes a suet pudding or two – but that's not the sort of thing that they do at Poplar Lodge. He teased me about not being there to see him. He said it just loud enough for Daniel to hear and I knew he was setting things up for me.

So he left us alone but before he did he told Martin to bring me my dessert and to bring Daniel one too. Martin didn't have to be told what to bring me because I have it every time I go there, but poor Daniel didn't have a clue what he'd be getting.

It was crème brûlée.

He said it was delicious. He said he'd never had it before. I saw that as my opening and I asked him if he'd like to try something else that he'd never had before.

Me.

Don't look at me like that. I was only doing what my father had told me to do. Well, he might not have said the exact words but I knew what he meant.

I thought at first that Daniel was going to say no. Nobody had ever said no before, but maybe Daniel was different. Maybe he would.

But it turned out he was just like the rest. He didn't say no and we went to The Marsden together. It's not the best hotel but it was handy. We registered as Mr and Mrs Smith but you could tell from the look on the receptionist's face that he didn't fall for it. Not that we cared. Daniel paid for one night bed and breakfast but we were only there a couple of hours. They probably changed the bed and sold the room again.

What a couple of hours they were, though! I'm going to be honest here and tell you that Daniel wasn't the first man I had ever been to bed with but I think you've probably guessed that. Not my first, but certainly my best, and I would never have believed it if I hadn't experienced it myself. He was considerate about my needs as well as his own and no-one else had ever done that before. I was used to men who only cared about themselves.

It was quite funny really because despite me being so much younger than him I was the one with more experience. He was so nervous and I thought he was going to have a heart attack when I sat on top of him as he lay in the bed. Poor Daniel didn't know what the hell was happening but I soon showed him what to do. He'd probably never realised that he could do it twice so close together.

I'm sorry; I shouldn't be talking like this should I? Not lady like at all, but you did ask and I've never claimed to be a lady. Plus, the truth is that I like sex. What's wrong with that? Just because I'm a woman I'm not supposed to enjoy it? You know, it wouldn't surprise me if, in the future, more women admit to enjoying it. I'm just ahead of my time, that's all.

In Daniel I'd found someone who understood me.

Before we left the room I thanked him for making me feel special and he looked so pleased with himself.

He really was very sweet.

Before we left the room, I thanked him for making me feel special and he looked so pleased with himself.
He really was very sweet.

DANIEL

'Is everything alright, darling?' Isobel asked me the following morning as we sat across the table from each other eating boiled eggs and soldiers. I know what we ate for a fact because after rationing finished we had boiled eggs and soldiers every morning for breakfast. Isobel said that she wanted to make up for all the powdered egg that she'd been forced to suffer.

So, like I said, she asked me if everything was alright.

'Yes,' I said, 'why shouldn't it be?' I gave the soggy white bread more attention than it deserved. It was either that or look my wife in the eye and I couldn't bring myself to do that.

'It's just that you seemed a little restless during the night,' she said, 'which isn't like you at all.' She started to pour herself another cup of tea but stopped with the tea pot in the air. 'Do you remember the night that you slept through the air raid siren?' She smiled as she thought about it and so did I. We had laughed for days after it happened. 'There's nothing wrong, is there?' she asked as she poured the liquid into her cup.

'No,' I lied. I pushed my chair back and stood up. I thanked her for my breakfast and said I had to go to work. I hadn't been able to look at her once. I didn't dare for fear that she would see the guilt I was feeling written all over my face.

56

I entered my office more than half an hour before the bank was due to open. My afternoon in bed with Lucy had come at a cost to my workload and I had some catching up to do.

I knew I might also have some explaining to do. Young Bridge had known about the lunch date with Arthur Braithwaite and had made a point of asking me if I would be coming back to the office.

'Of course I will,' I'd said and I'd been confident that I would be. I'd expected to spend a couple of hours with my newest client and be back in time to try and come up with a repayment schedule for a man who wanted to buy his first car. I hadn't bargained on Lucy turning up and her father leaving us alone. And I certainly hadn't bargained on her offering herself to me on a plate.

She had offered herself, hadn't she? And I am only human after all. What red blooded man would have turned her down? It's a question I'd asked myself a thousand times the night before as I was laying on my back staring at the ceiling while I thought Isobel was asleep beside me. She hadn't moved from her sleeping position all night, which meant she had been facing the wall with her back to me. It was how she slept every night, so how was I to know that night was any different?

However, in my office, in the cold light of day, I thought about what I had done. I caught myself smiling at one point and had to drag my mind back from the warmth of Lucy's naked body underneath those crisp white sheets. She had been so eager and willing, but there had been

57

something else, something that I hadn't been able to put my finger on at first. She had experience.

The way she had undressed both herself and me, the way she had kissed me and the way she had caressed me all bore the hallmarks of practice. She hadn't been a virgin, of that I was sure, and if I had to guess I would say that she had had more lovers than me. After all, three's not a very large number, is it?

Stop it! Stop it! Stop it! I screamed the words silently, holding my head in my hands. I grabbed some hair between my fingers and pulled. I had to do something to stop myself thinking about what I had done the day before.

I shouldn't have done it, I knew that. I had betrayed my wife and I had let both myself and my employers down. Forming friendships with clients wasn't encouraged in case it affected one's ability to be objective, and I was certain that would extend to the daughters of clients.

That was when the thought hit me. *Oh my God.* She wouldn't have told him, would she? She wouldn't have told her dad how we'd spent the afternoon. Would she? The thought that she may have made me sweat and suddenly I was struggling to breathe. I loosened my tie and took deep breaths through the hand that I had over my mouth and I thought for a second that I was going to be sick.

I didn't know what to do. I mean, I'd never done anything like this before and I couldn't help wondering how my life had suddenly become so complicated.

Two weeks ago Arthur Braithwaite was just a name, a man I'd read about in newspapers. I knew next to nothing about him other than he owned three factories in the town, all manufacturing different things, ensuring that he had a strangle hold over the community. Over half of everything that was manufactured in the town came out of a factory owned by Arthur Braithwaite. He was a very successful businessman but there were some shady rumours about how he achieved that success. Once, a few years back, there had been talk in the papers about a link to some gangster from London, but that had died down as quickly as it had surfaced. I remember laughing at the use of the word 'gangster' when I'd read the article to Isobel. 'It's not bloody Chicago,' I'd said.

Those words came back to haunt me because whatever they called themselves I was sure that my new 'friend' knew some very unsavoury characters. I didn't dwell on what those characters might do to me. The room started to spin and I thought I was going to faint. I sat with my arms on my desk and my head resting in my hands and asked myself why I had allowed myself to get caught up in this mess.

I didn't care what Morris or anyone said – there was something fishy about the whole loan thing. In all my years I'd never known anything like the deal that we had done. *We had done. We.* I was one of them. I was part of it. I was complicit. I wondered if I should I have gone to the board and told them what happened, told them what I had been asked to do.

I've asked myself a hundred times why I didn't tell someone and it always comes back to the carrot that Morris had dangled in front of me. The seat behind the desk at the High Street branch is the job that I had dreamed of for the last five years.

But I could kiss goodbye to it if Arthur Braithwaite complained to the shareholders that I had slept with his daughter. What if he told them that I had seduced Lucy? She was a very young woman, little more than a girl really, and I was a much older man. Anyone would believe him and even if they didn't he had enough influence to make the mud stick. My career, not to mention my marriage, would be over.

Isobel is the polar opposite to Lucy. She would never have gone to bed with a man that she barely knew. She would never go to bed with a man that she wasn't married to. In all the years that we've been married I've never seen Isobel totally naked. Even during our infrequent lovemaking there has always been a Winceyette nightgown between us. Floral prints are her particular favourite, with high collars and sleeves that go all the way to the wrist. 'Passion Killers' my friends call them, and they're not wrong. I've never added anything to those particular conversations. I didn't want anyone to know anything about our private life so I've just kept quiet and laughed along with them.

But her lack of interest in that side of marriage didn't make Isobel a bad wife. To be fair to her she never turned me down, it's just that she seemed quite happy for me not to ask that often. I would have been happy to ask more regularly but I've never liked the idea of forcing her to do something that she doesn't like. She just doesn't enjoy that sort of thing in the way that Lucy clearly does.

In all other respects Isobel is the perfect wife. The house is always perfectly clean and there is always a meal on the table for me when I get home from work. She has never overspent on her housekeeping allowance and she has kept a good home. All in all she is a good wife.

So why had I slept with Lucy?

I was still asking myself that question and coming up with no answer when I heard the sound of voices outside my door. Two voices, Johnson and Bridge. Quickly I straightened my tie and stroked my hair back into place.

There was a discreet knock at the door.

'Yes.'

The door opened and Anthony Bridge popped his head around the door quickly followed by the rest of his body. Johnson was just inches behind him.

'Can I get you anything, Mr Laither?' Johnson asked, as if he needed a reason to be there.

'Mm, yes, yes please Johnson.' I stuttered. 'Get me the Potter file will you.'

'Of course sir,' I read his lips because I swear the words didn't actually come out.

I saw Johnson glance at Bridge as he left the room and closed the door behind him.

My assistant turned his attention to me. He stood just inches from the door, square shouldered with his chin jutting out in front of him. There was something slightly comical about the stance but I wasn't in the mood for laughing. I looked at the clock on the wall above his head. Fifteen minutes until opening time.

'Can I help you Mr Bridge?' I asked.

'I just wondered how the meeting had gone yesterday,' he said. 'I expected you back by the afternoon so when you weren't I was afraid that there was something wrong.'

'No, nothing wrong,' I said slowly, giving myself time to think. 'The lunch just lasted longer than I had anticipated. It wasn't really a meeting at all.'

'I was concerned that there might have been a problem.' I don't know if I've mentioned this before but Bridge is a bit like a dog with a bone, and once he's onto something he won't let it lie. I was grateful when there was another knock on the door and Johnson walked in holding a thick folder.

'Here's the file you wanted, Mr Laither,' he said as he placed it on the desk in front of me.

'Thank you very much, Mr Johnson.' I opened the folder and said, 'I'm expecting Mr Potter about ten o'clock, would you show him straight in please?'

'Yes sir,'

I turned my attention back to Bridge, who was still standing to the left of my desk. 'Is there anything else I can help you with Mr Bridge?' I knew that my tone was a little curt but I really didn't care.

'No,' Bridge's tone was equally curt. 'I'll be at my desk if you need me.' He didn't bother trying to hide a smirk from his face. He can read situations. He had known where I was going and he had known who I was going to meet.

He had already voiced his reservations about the deal that I had done with Braithwaite and I couldn't help thinking that he was waiting for everything to implode. After what I had done the day before he might not have to wait too long.

They both gave a little bow and prepared to leave. I watched the door close behind them and let out a deep breath when they were gone.

I went about my business for the rest of the day, just about managing to keep my mind on the job while keeping one eye on the door just in case Lucy's father walked through it. By the close of business, when there was still no sign of him, I started to relax. Lucy hadn't told him.

All that was left to do was go home.

As usual Isobel was there to greet me when I walked through the door and I was comforted by it. The day before had been a moment of weakness, maybe even madness, but now my world was how it should be. Or at least it was until we went to bed.

We had had a lovely evening together; we listened to the radio and chatted until about ten o'clock before retiring for the night. As I lay beside her, I was drawn to her and I initiated love making.

Isobel seemed different that night, not as keen as Lucy had been but certainly receptive to my advances. The next thing I knew I'd almost put my tongue in her mouth just like I had with Lucy. I didn't realise I'd done it until it was too late but I stopped as quick as I could and I think I got away with it.

The following morning Mrs Warren knocked on the door and came into my office carrying a tray. It was ten thirty and she was bringing me a cup of tea like she had every morning at that time since the day I'd started. She balanced the tray on the palm of one hand as she put the cup and saucer to the right of my blotter. My head was down as I read some papers but when she didn't leave I looked up.

'This just came for you,' she said. She was holding a small blue box in her hand.

'What is it?' I asked. She said she didn't know. I asked her why she hadn't opened it. I thought it was a reasonable enough question because, as she'd pointed out to Anthony Bridge, she opens all of my mail.

Apparently it wasn't a reasonable question because she raised an eyebrow and said, 'Because I thought it looked like a gift.'

She was right, it did. I remember moving it around in my hands, just looking at it. I was confused. I mean, who on earth would be sending me a present? It wasn't my birthday, but even if it was, no-one would send me a gift to the office. There was no-one to send me a gift. Isobel gave me socks every birthday which she would wrap in brown paper and hand to me while we were having breakfast, and my mother would give me a hand knitted jumper just as it was. To be honest I wish she wouldn't bother because she has arthritis in her hands and she seems to drop more stitches than she knits. Sorry, you didn't need to know that. I'll get back to the present that I was holding in my hands.

Like I said, I was confused. I looked up to see that Mrs Warren looked just as confused as I did. 'Who brought it?' I asked.

'A man in a suit,' she said with a shrug of her shoulders. 'Apparently he just came up to the front desk and asked if Daniel Laither was in. When Mr Johnson said that you were, the man asked if this could be passed on to you.'

That hadn't cleared anything up. I looked at the box again and noticed that my hands were shaking. If Mrs Warren noticed, and she would have because she misses nothing, she didn't say anything.

I placed the box on the desk and pulled the ribbon. The paper opened to reveal a box with the name of a local jewellers shop embossed in gold letters across the top. I looked at Mrs Warren and saw that she was looking at me, urging me on with her eyes to hurry up and get the box opened.

I lifted the lid and revealed the contents.

Mrs Warren strained her neck to see what was inside. 'A watch?' She sounded as surprised as I felt. 'Who would send you a watch?'

'I don't know,' I could hear something in my voice that I thought sounded like fear. I could only think of one person who might have sent the watch to me and he was the last person on earth that I wanted to be giving me expensive presents. In my world they are called bribes and I wanted nothing to do with them.

I lifted it out of the box so that I could take a closer look. I ran my fingers around its large face where the numbers were etched in gold. It had a rim of matching gold around its circumference and the word 'Smiths' underneath the number twelve. I fingered the brown leather strap.

'Is there a card?' Mrs Warren asked. I checked the box and found that that there wasn't. 'What about the back?' She suggested. 'Is there an inscription?'

There was. Two words, 'thank you.'

'Who can it be from?' She whispered.

'I don't know,' I said, but I had a sickening feeling that I did.

'If you were to ask me,' she said, 'I'd say that it's from Mr Braithwaite.'

'Do you think so?' I tried to make it sound like the idea had never occurred to me.

'I typed the contract, remember?' She looked at me and I swear I saw compassion in her eyes like she sensed that I had got myself into something that I shouldn't have. 'He must think a lot of you,' she said as she turned to walk away.

I forced another smile. I didn't want Arthur Braithwaite to think a lot of me. I didn't really want him to think of me at all.

The next day I was just returning to my office after lunch when I heard the phone on Mrs Warren's desk ring. 'Good afternoon, Mr Laither's secretary, how may I help you?' she said with her usual efficiency. She listened a second or two before saying, 'Mr Laither was at lunch, I'll just check if he's back yet. May I ask who's calling please?' She nodded her head, maintaining eye contact with me all of the time. 'One moment please.' She pressed the button that put the caller on hold and said, 'they won't give a name, said it was a private matter.'

I wasn't alarmed because clients sometimes did that sort of thing. 'You'd better put them through,' I said opening the door to the office. By the time I'd closed it the phone on my desk was ringing and I picked it up on the third ring. 'Daniel Laither,' I said as I sat down, 'can I ask who I am speaking to please.'

'Guess.'

I didn't need to guess, 'Miss Braithwaite,' I said formally, 'how are you?' I was thinking of her as the daughter of a client rather than a woman that I had spent a couple of sweet hours in bed with a few days earlier.

'Miss Braithwaite?' she said. 'I thought you and I were on first name terms, Daniel.' Her voice was slow and sultry.

'How are you... Lucy?' I have to confess I liked the way that her name sounded.

'That's better,' she giggled, 'I'm fine thank you. How are you?'

'Very well,' I said, 'thank you.' It was all very polite. I know I am a pathetic excuse for a man but I loved the fact that she was interested in me. Flattered I suppose.

'Where did you go for lunch?' Her voice was so light and breezy that I couldn't help smiling.

'Excuse me?' It struck me as an odd question.

'Your secretary said you were out to lunch,' she explained. 'Where did you go? Or is that what she says to everyone who rings you?'

'I think she maybe does use it as an excuse sometimes,' I confided, though God knows why. 'But no, I was at lunch.'

'So where did you go?' she persisted.

I couldn't see a reason not to tell her so I said, 'To the café at the end of the road.'

'Do you go there a lot?' I didn't understand why she wanted to know but I couldn't help being pleased that she did.

'Now and then,' I admitted. There was a pause in the conversation and all I could hear was her breathing into the phone. 'I'm sorry Lucy,' I said. 'But I have a meeting in ten minutes.'

'I'll not keep you then,' she said. 'I just rang to see if you liked your present?'

'My present?' I wondered if I had heard her right.

'Yes, your present.' There was a hint of something in her voice, it might have been concern. 'You did get the watch didn't you?'

'I thought it was from your father.' I don't know why I said that, other than it was the truth. I hadn't yet become comfortable lying.

'Daddy?' I could hear her laughing and I realised that it was a ridiculous notion. 'No Daniel, the watch was from me. Just a little thank you for the lovely afternoon that we spent together.' I was opening my mouth but no words

68

came out. 'Anyway,' she said lightly, 'I don't want to keep you from your meeting. Bye Daniel. See you soon.'

The phone went dead and I slowly replaced the receiver into the base.

Lucy had sent the watch. I hadn't expected that.

LUCY

Daniel looked so sweet, standing on the pavement outside the hotel waving at me as my taxi drove away. He really is a lovely man, so kind and considerate. He had made me feel so special and I wasn't used to that, not by anyone other than my father anyway. I'm used to men who take me out to dinner in posh restaurants just to try and impress me enough to go to bed with them. I'm used to men who like to brag to their mates that they've 'had' me. Before Daniel I'd never known a man who cared how I felt, and I felt a little bad that we were using him.

One of the first things that my father taught me was that there are two types of people. Them and us. He also taught me that we use *them* to get what *we* want. The key was not to let them know they were being used. And, let's be honest, Daniel wasn't complaining, he probably thought he'd died and gone to Heaven.

He had been easy enough to get to the hotel so we already had something that we would be able to hold over him, but we needed more than one afternoon in bed. That was when I came up with the idea of the watch. Coming from my father it could have been construed as a bribe but if I bought it, it would be a present, a thank you present. I came up with the idea myself but I thought that my father would have approved. The way I saw it, Daniel's wife wouldn't look too kindly on him accepting expensive gifts

70

from strange women. I thought that I could use that to keep him under control. I mean, if he grew a conscience and wanted to end our arrangement I could use it against him and threaten to tell his wife. Once my father gave me the nod I would send him back to his normal life, but until then I needed him to keep playing the game. The watch was just a means to an end.

I'd told the taxi driver where to take me. I wanted to go to the jewellers on Grant Street. I asked the driver to pull over and told him to wait for me while I went inside. My father buys all of my mother's jewellery there and the staff all know me.

At that point I hadn't decided on exactly what I wanted other than something expensive so I told the lady behind the counter, I think she's called Janet, that I wanted a gift for a man. She suggested cuff links but I didn't like that idea. Everybody buys a man cufflinks when they can't think of anything more original. My father must have a million pairs of them.

When I looked along the glass counter and saw the watches I knew that was what I would buy. It didn't take me long to find the one that I wanted. It had a gold rim around the face and a brown leather strap. It was also the most expensive one they had. Janet asked if I wanted it engraved and I was sure that I did though it took me a couple of minutes to decide what I wanted it to say. Eventually I settled on *Thank You*. I thought that was clever because how would he explain that away? There was a small chance that he would refuse it and then my plan would blow up in my face, but I wasn't too worried about that. If there's one thing I know, its men.

Janet asked if I wanted it wrapping and I thought why not, it was a gift after all and I have to say that she did a much better job of it than I ever could have. Do you think that they have to have special training in wrapping things to work in a shop like that?

I didn't have any money with me so I charged it to my father's account. I've done that before when I've been buying a present for one of my friends so it wasn't a problem, and anyway, I didn't think he would mind me buying a present for Daniel.

My mother was in the lounge when I got home. She caught sight of the bag that I was holding and asked me what was in it.

'Just a present,' I said.

'Expensive present,' she nodded towards the bag. It was none of her business so I just shrugged my shoulders. I had started to walk away when she said, 'Shall I tell your father that he can expect the bill?'

I ignored her and carried on walking. I'm used to that sort of thing from her. She spends enough of my father's money but she hates it when I do. Basically she is jealous of me because my father loves me more than he does her.

I don't know why I just told you that.

Anyway, I took the watch upstairs to my bedroom and just sat on the bed for a long time holding it. I had to plan what I was going to do next.

I had to come up with the best way of giving Daniel the watch.

I thought of going to the bank and dropping it off myself but I quickly dismissed that idea because I didn't want our relationship to be common knowledge. It would be most effective if it was as a secret because, you see, the thing about secrets is that you don't want anyone to find out. If you have a secret that's bad enough then you will do almost anything to keep it and that's what I was relying on.

In the end I asked Robert to take it for me.

Robert has worked for my father for years and he's known me since I was born. I can ask Robert to do anything for me and he'll do it without asking any questions. In some respects he's just like an obedient dog.

When my father came home I asked him if Robert would be able to do a favour for me the following day.

'Of course he can,' he said. 'Just ring Alice in the morning and tell her what you need.'

I told him that I had bought Daniel a present and you know what he said? 'Good girl.'

I rang the office the next morning and Alice Monroe sounded annoyed when I told her to send Robert round to the house. 'I'll need to check that he's not doing something for your father,' she said and I enjoyed telling her that my father was the one who had told me to ring. I think I heard her make a little noise but I let it go because at the end of the day my father loves me and I don't think she can say the same. She might be his mistress but I don't think she means any more to him that any of the other women he's slept with, and I think she knows that. I feel a bit sorry for her really.

Robert arrived at the house less than half an hour later. I gave him the box and told him where I wanted it to be delivered to.

He rang me about an hour later to say that it had been done.

I waited in the house all day thinking that Daniel would ring to say thank you but he didn't. Every time the telephone rang I expected it to be him but it never was. By the following afternoon I was starting to worry. I wasn't worried that he didn't like it; I mean who wouldn't like a watch that cost more than a lot of people earned in a year? I was worried that he had remembered his wife and refused the gift. I didn't worry about it too long though because I honestly couldn't see that being the case. I decided it was probably because he just didn't know how to thank me.

I decided to ring him. My father gave me what I thought was Daniel's direct number except it wasn't direct and I got that woman, his secretary instead. She said that Daniel was at lunch and she would see if he was back yet. How could she not know if he was back yet? Her desk is about three feet from his office door. I thought she probably told everyone that he was at lunch, but only if it was lunchtime, obviously. She probably had a range of excuses to fit various times of day. She asked me who I was but I didn't tell her. I'm sorry, but it was none of her business. She put me on hold for a couple of seconds and then the phone rang again. This time Daniel picked it up.

If I'm honest it was nice to hear his voice again because it's all deep and masculine, just like a matinee idol. He called me Miss Braithwaite again and I put that down to him being at work but after what we had been doing earlier in the week I didn't think there was any need so be so formal.

He seemed surprised when I asked him if he liked the watch. I don't think he'd even realised it was from me. I wondered who else he thought might have sent it to him.

DANIEL

The phone call from Lucy took me totally by surprise. That the watch had come from her had never occurred to me. When I saw it I'd immediately thought it came from her father and when I'd read the inscription on the back I'd been sure of it. I'd thought he was being a smug bugger, you know, throwing his money around, showing me once again how rich and important he was. It seemed like just the sort of thing that he would do. But it had come from Lucy; she was the one thanking me.

It really was a beautiful thing and I would have been really proud to wear it, but I just couldn't see how I would ever be able to do that. First of all, anyone would be able to see that it was something that I couldn't afford to buy myself. And secondly, I couldn't admit who had bought it for me.

I realised that Lucy and I had yet another secret, and while that felt a little uncomfortable, the bigger feeling I had was excitement.

Once I'd realised who had sent the watch I should have refused to accept it, I should have sent it back but I didn't. To do that would be to acknowledge that we had done something wrong.

I didn't see or hear from Lucy for the next couple of weeks, though I thought about her a fair bit. Christmas was just around the corner and I thought it might be nice if I bought her a present. It wouldn't be anything as grand as the watch she had bought me because my salary from the bank didn't run to that kind of thing, but I wanted to buy her something, a small token of our friendship.

But you have to imagine that Lucy would have everything that she wanted, her father would have seen to that. So what on earth do you buy the person with everything? In the end I settled on a bracelet. It was a thin gold band with green stones in it. I had no idea what they were; all I knew was that it was the only piece of jewellery that I could realistically afford. The first lesson I learned when I started working at the bank was that a man must live within his means.

I bought Isobel a box of talcum powder and a pair of gloves that cost a fraction of what the bracelet had cost me. Even then I realised that the bracelet had a moral cost as well as a financial one.

Once I'd bought the bracelet I didn't know what to do with it. How was I supposed to get it to her? I could hardly turn up at her house. Not unless I wanted to be answering some serious questions from her father. Likewise I couldn't post it because I imagined she would then be the one answering the questions.

Was I being silly? Probably. I look back now and wonder what the hell I was playing at, but I just couldn't help myself. She had this hold on me. I thought about her all the time. On the rare occasions that Isobel and I made love it was Lucy that I was thinking about and I hated myself for that. Isobel deserved better.

But knowing that didn't change anything. I still couldn't help thinking about Lucy and, if I'm being honest, I knew that, given the chance, I would be with her again, you know, in an intimate way.

I kept the bracelet in the bottom drawer of my desk at work, the one that I keep locked. I couldn't risk putting it in one of the others because Mrs Warren might find it and I couldn't take it home in case Isobel found it. I had to put it in a secret place. Just one more in a lengthening list of secrets. And that in itself should have told me I was doing something wrong.

Sometime in the middle of December I had a meeting with Arthur Braithwaite and I spent the entire morning preparing for it. Not that there was a lot of preparation required because it was more of a courtesy follow up, really.

From what I understand, when Mr Braithwaite's secretary had called to make the appointment she'd told Mrs Warren that her employer 'liked to keep abreast of everything that is going on.'

Mrs Warren hadn't really understood the need for the meeting any more than I had. It wasn't customary after a loan was set up, as long as they kept up the repayments, and to her way of thinking it was a waste of time. She said as much when she wrote it in my diary.

'There's just something about that man that I don't like,' she said, 'and I don't understand why he needs to come here and see you.'

'He's just a very thorough business man.' I defended him even though I agreed with her.

'Usually, once they've got their money you don't see them for dust.' Mrs Warren had worked for the bank for a long time and knew what she was talking about. She noticed the empty cup and saucer on my desk and asked me if I would like a refill.

'No thank you Ida,' I pushed the chair back and stood up. 'I think I'll go to lunch now.'

I grabbed my overcoat from its peg behind the door and put it on as I walked.

Once I got outside I lifted the collar of my coat up around my ears though it was more from habit than for the effect it would have in the time it took me to walk the distance from the bank to the café on the corner.

The bell above the door rang as I opened it and hot air caused my glasses to steam up briefly.

'What'll it be today, Mr Laither?' Mrs Holden asked. I couldn't see her through my clouded glasses but I recognised her voice.

'What's the soup today?' I was happy to see that my preferred table by the window was free and I sat down with my back to the glass.

'Ham broth,' she said, 'Mr Walker had some hocks in his window yesterday,' she dipped her head in the general direction of the butcher's, 'so I said to my Alf, "I'm having some of them for broth."'

'Ham broth it is then please, Mrs Holden,' I was already looking forward to it even as I asked for it. Mrs Holden's soup is legendary in these parts.

'Coming right up Mr Laither.' She laughed, probably because she hadn't needed to ask.

As she went off to prepare my food I sat back and looked at the other people in the café. It wasn't a big place, just ten tables, but only another two of them were taken. A man and woman sat at the table in the corner and there was a man on his own sitting at the one nearest the till. All three of them appeared to be having a bowl of the broth but it was that sort of day. Damp and miserable days called for comforting food.

I was sorry to see the place so empty. Mrs Holden made good food and sold it at a good price. It was a sound business model and she deserved to be doing better. The mortgage on it has about three years to run and as I sat there I hoped she and Alf would be able to see it through. The thought of foreclosing on it left a heavy feeling in the pit of my stomach.

The couple left before my food arrived and I was less than a quarter of the way down my bowl of broth when the man by the till got up to leave too.

I didn't notice the man holding the door open for anyone to come in so I didn't realise that Lucy was there until she pulled out a chair and sat down.

'Hello Daniel,' she purred.

I looked up from my bowl and I know my eyes flicked around the room to make sure that no-one else had come in without me noticing it. 'Hello Lucy.'

She turned around in her chair and said. 'Could I have a bowl of whatever Daniel's having please?'

I saw Mrs Holden look up and nod her head but she didn't say anything.

Lucy turned back to face me. 'I almost didn't see you,' she said, playfully tapping the arm I had resting on the table. 'Who sits at a window table with their back to it? You are funny, Daniel.' Her eyes sparkled as she smiled at me and I felt myself being drawn into them.

The spell was broken when Mrs Holden arrived carrying a bowl of broth in one hand and a spoon in the other. She set them down in front of Lucy. 'Will there be anything else Miss?' she asked. Lucy shook her head and smiled at her. I noticed that it wasn't anywhere near as broad as the smile that she had given me. 'Mr Laither?' I think it was a couple of seconds before I realised I was being spoken to.

I coughed and said, 'Thank you Mrs Holden, I'm fine.'

She went back to the counter with her slippers shuffling as she walked.

I watched Lucy as she ate. She seemed to be enjoying it and I wondered if she had ever eaten ham broth before. I doubted that she had. For a slim girl she really knew how to eat! I could feel myself smiling as I watched her devour her food.

'What was that?' she asked as she scraped the last few drops off the bottom of the bowl.

I told her that it was ham broth and she said that it was good.

'Just what you need on a day like today,' I said. It was a struggle to keep my tone flat because I was feeling giddy inside.

Lucy placed her spoon inside the empty bowl and rested her elbows on the table. She leaned forward. 'I was hoping you'd be here,' she said. I didn't know what to say so I said nothing. 'I've been thinking about you.' I still didn't trust myself to say anything so I just looked at her as she asked. 'Have you been thinking about me?'

'Yes,' I admitted, but I didn't tell her how much.

Mrs Holden arrived to clear our plates and we were silent until she was out of earshot.

Lucy lowered her head and looked at me from under her fringe. 'Have you been thinking about that afternoon?'

'Yes.' Why lie about it? If I'd said anything else she would have known that I was lying. I swallowed hard.

'Would you like to do it again?'

I wanted to scream *Oh God yes please* but something grabbed me, guilt probably. As I stared at her my teeth were clamped firmly together and I could feel the muscles in my cheeks twitch under the strain. I took care to control my breathing.

'We can't.' I had to force the words out.

'Why not?' she had a disappointed look in her eyes and a pout on her lips and I recognised it as the look of a person who wasn't used to hearing the word no.

'Because we can't.' I tried to sound like I meant it but I didn't even convince myself.

'That's not a reason, Daniel,' she leaned forward and tilted her head to one side. I watched her tongue flick out of her mouth and her teeth move over her lower lip. She looked at me and spoke slowly, 'So I'll ask you again. Why can't we?'

I leaned forwards too so that our heads were only a few inches apart. Mrs Holden was behind the counter and pretending to dry a plate, and even though I'm pretty sure that she's a bit deaf I didn't want to take the chance of being overheard. 'Because,' I said just as slowly, 'you are the daughter of one of my clients.'

'Well he's the bank's client really, Daniel,' she said lightly and I nodded my head sideways, acknowledging she was right.

'You are the daughter of one of the bank's clients,' I corrected myself.

'Don't worry about my father,' she said as she looked me straight in the eyes. I could see that something was going on in that pretty little head of hers as she looked like she was weighing something up, like she was choosing her words carefully. She settled on, 'Daddy hates to see me unhappy.'

Did he? Of course he did. She was his princess and he treated her like one. Her father had made a point of telling me how much Lucy meant to him. So what did she mean by *Daddy hates to see me unhappy*? I'm not stupid, well I know you might disagree, but what I mean is I knew exactly what she meant. If I said no she would tell her father about us.

I know what you're thinking because I'm thinking that myself now. I should have been strong. I should have said no and walked away. Instead I sat opposite her and allowed myself to be drawn further and further into the mess I had fallen into.

'You *would* like to see me again, wouldn't you Daniel?' She rested her chin on her hand and looked at me in such a way that I would have done anything for her.

'Yes.' I wasn't lying. I'd already admitted to myself that I wanted to be with her again. Even though I knew it was wrong, I knew that I wanted to feel the way she made me feel again. What man wouldn't?

'Good.' She sat back in her chair and watched her finger as she ran it up and down the salt cellar. 'I'm so pleased to hear you say that. I had such a good time.' She lifted her eyes but not her head and looked at me.

'So did I,' I admitted. Like I've said, why lie to her? She was perfectly aware of the effect that she had on me.

She smiled at me again and I couldn't help but smile back. Just being near her made me happy. Her eyes broke away from mine, dropping down to focus on my mouth, my jaw, my chest, my wrist...

'Where's your watch?' she asked.

'At home.' I said, putting my hand under the table.

'Don't you like it?' She made me feel like a naughty schoolboy.

84

'Of course I do,' I said, 'it's just that it's special. It's not the sort of watch to be worn every day.' The answer seemed to please her, or at least placate her, and her face softened. I put my hand back on the table and looked at the watch I was wearing, the one that Isobel had bought me for my fortieth birthday. 'I have to go,' I said.

'Oh.' She looked genuinely surprised.

'I'm due back,' as I said it I realised that she probably had no concept of how a working day was made up. 'I have one hour for lunch and I've been gone fifty five minutes.'

'But you're the boss.' She really was so naïve in some respects.

'So I have to set an example,' I explained.

'That's just what my father says.'

I wondered what sort of example Arthur Braithwaite set to his employees.

LUCY

So Daniel had thought that the watch had come from my father. Once I realised that, it gave me something else to play with.

After that phone call I didn't do anything for a couple of weeks. I needed to give Daniel time to dwell on what he had gotten himself into. I knew that he'd be thinking about me, maybe even dreaming about me, and that was exactly what I was relying on.

I thought about him too, but only in regards to what my next step should be. I had enjoyed the time we spent in the hotel bedroom and I wouldn't mind doing it again but I knew that I would need more than that if we were to keep Daniel where we wanted him.

I would let his wife have his attention for a couple of weeks because soon she'd be getting less and less of it.

I did spare a thought for his wife, you know, the one he hadn't told me he had. Despite what you might think I'm not a home breaker. After all, I'm not the one who's married. If his wife really meant anything to him Daniel would have said no.

What am I saying? That was never going to happen.

My father caught me over breakfast one day, I think it was the week after I'd phoned the bank, and asked me how

86

Daniel was. Well no, that's not true. He asked how *Danny* was.

Has Daniel already told you that my father always called him Danny? He has, hasn't he? Of course he would. He hates it and my father knows that. Right back at the beginning my father said that I was to call him Daniel but *he* always made a point of calling him Danny.

So what he actually said that morning was, 'How's Danny?'

'I haven't seen him for a couple of weeks,' I said, 'but he seemed fine then.'

'How did he like the present you bought him?' He asked as he threw the last of his breakfast tea into his mouth.

I laughed as I told him that Daniel hadn't realised the watch was from me. 'He thought it was from you.'

My father nearly spat his tea out as he laughed too.

'Will you be seeing him again?' my father asked as he stood up from the table.

'What do you think?' I asked.

He smiled at me, kissed the top of my head, and said he would see me later.

After the door had closed behind him, my mother finally lifted her head from the magazine that she had been pretending to read and asked, 'Is that the bank manager Danny that you were talking about?' I didn't get the chance to reply before she asked her next question. 'Why are you buying the bank manager presents?' and the next, 'and what did your father mean by "will you be seeing him again?"'

It really had nothing to do with her but I was sick of all the questions. 'Yes,' I snapped, 'it's the bank manager. But his name is Daniel, not Danny. I've met him a few times and we get along.' I got up from my seat because I didn't want to get into a conversation with her.

She closed the magazine and put it on the table. 'And do you buy presents for everyone you get along with?'

She mimicked my voice which was very annoying and I didn't hide that annoyance as I said, 'It was his birthday.'

I don't know if she believed me but it did shut her up which had been the intention.

I gave it another few days and decided that he had had long enough to think about things. My father had told me that he would be seeing Daniel again but I didn't want to hijack another meeting. Given that I'd done that twice before he was probably expecting it. I had to do something that he wasn't expecting. Expect the unexpected, that's what my father's always saying, and as I lay in bed one night it came to me.

When I'd telephoned him at the bank a couple of weeks earlier he said that he'd been out to lunch and when I asked him where he had been he said to the café on the corner. I decided that I would go there to see if I could find him.

I remembered the time that I had called the bank when that woman had said she would see if he was back. You had to assume that Daniel took his lunch break at a regular time every day because he's just that sort of person, so I worked out that he must have his lunch about twelve thirty.

The following day I made my way down to the café on the corner. It was the sort of place I wouldn't be seen dead in, so I just pretended to read the menu pasted on the window, but really I was looking past the yellowing paper for Daniel. He wasn't there. But that wouldn't deter me – I had a plan and I was sticking to it.

On the second day I did the exact same thing, and there he was, sitting in the window seat facing into the café. His shoulders were hunched as he ate but I recognised him straight away.

This was the last place he would expect to see me.

I'd never been into anywhere like it before. The cafés I normally visited had nice table cloths, whereas this one had chipped oilcloth. Why would Daniel come here? Surely a bank manager could afford something better. Maybe that was his mother behind the counter, though I hoped not.

A man was coming out so I managed to sneak in without the bell over the door ringing. I went to Daniel's table and stood there. He looked surprised to see me as I pulled out the other chair and sat down. I asked the woman behind the counter to bring me a bowl of whatever it was that Daniel was having. He said that it was ham broth. When I'd ordered it I hadn't thought I'd be able to eat anything that had been made in that place but I scoffed the lot.

Eating gave me time to think.

I gave him my flirtiest look because that's never failed to get me what I want from a man. I told him that I had

89

been thinking about him and asked if he'd been thinking about me. He said that he had. I told him how much I had enjoyed our afternoon together and I asked him if he would like to do it again, but he said we couldn't. Damn, had he actually grown a conscience? I thought that was when he was going to tell me he was married, but he didn't. He said it was because my father was his client. I pointed out that my father was really the bank's client, not his, so that wasn't an excuse.

'Being with you again like we were would make me happy Daniel,' I said. I know I sound like I was being coy but I thought that he would prefer that to the coarse language I sometimes use with my girlfriends.

'It would make me happy too Lucy,' he said, 'but I have to think of your father.'

'Then you'd best make me happy Daniel, because Daddy doesn't like it when I'm not.' It was just a statement of fact but I knew it might have sounded like I was threatening him.

In a way I was.

Eventually he admitted that he would like to see me again.

With that finally out of the way I could turn my attention to what I had noticed almost as soon as I had sat down. I asked him why he wasn't wearing his watch. Of course I knew why he wasn't wearing it. After all, Daniel needing to keep the watch a secret had been the reason I'd bought it in the first place, but I made a big thing out of it not being on his wrist. The funny thing is that he immediately put his hand under the table, reminding me of a child that covers their eyes and thinks if they can't see you, you can't see them. I pretended to be upset and asked him if he didn't like it. He said he did like it but that he hadn't worn it because it was 'special.' He said it wasn't a watch to be worn every day. And while that's perfectly correct, I enjoyed watching him squirm as he came up with a believable reply.

Almost immediately he brought his hand out from under the table and looked at the watch that he was wearing. He said he had to get back to work. He spent a couple of minutes explaining why he had to get back. You know, I honestly think he thought I didn't realise how long a lunch hour is. I'm laughing because, despite appearances, I did rather well at school, but even if I hadn't I think I could have worked that one out.

We didn't make any arrangements to see each other again but I knew that we would, and it would be soon.

DANIEL

I wasn't surprised to see her in the café, sitting at the table we had sat at before. It was a couple of days later and although we hadn't made an arrangement to see each other again I had this feeling that she would be there and, despite the niggling feeling that she could be part of the game that her father was playing with me, I was happy to see her. I suppose I wanted to believe that she really was interested in me and not just there because it was part of Arthur Braithwaite's grand plan.

She was sitting in the same seat as she had before. She was looking out of the window at the people walking by. She had a cup of tea in front of her which she was sipping, and her face lit up when I came in. Her delight looked genuine enough to me. I sat down opposite her with my back to the window and immediately lost myself in her eyes. She'd laughed at me before for sitting with my back to the view outside, but why would I want to look out at the street when I could look at her?

'I told you that you needn't have worried, love,' Mrs Holden said as she came to the table, notepad in hand ready to take my order.

'Excuse me?' I wasn't sure which of us she was talking to.

Mrs Holden's pencil hovered over her pad as she explained. 'I'm just saying to the young lady here that I told her not to worry about you not coming in today. I've never known you to miss a Friday in I don't know how long.'

'Am I that predictable, Mrs Holden?' I laughed.

She didn't say anything but she gave me a look that told me I was.

We ordered sandwiches and a pot of tea for two and Mrs Holden waddled away to prepare our food.

'I didn't expect to see you here.' I said. I know I've just told you that I *did* expect it but I couldn't tell her that. Women hate to appear predictable.

'Why not?' she asked. Her head tilted to the side and her eyes were wide. Apparently I had quickly glanced around, though I didn't realise it until she mentioned it. 'Are you checking to see if anyone you know is here?' she asked.

'What?' Her question surprised me because, like I said, I hadn't realised that I had done it.

'You're looking around,' she giggled, 'like you're worried someone you know might see us.'

'No,' I tried to laugh it off, pretending that she hadn't hit the nail on the head, 'don't be silly.' Whether I'd realised what I was doing or not, it was one of the first things that crossed my mind.

We talked about nothing in particular to kill the time before the food arrived. Just chit chat, normal things, just like an ordinary couple who were meeting for lunch. Except we weren't a normal couple, were we? She was Lucy Braithwaite and I was married.

93

Why hadn't I told her that I was married the other day? Why hadn't I said *we can't do it again Lucy because I'm married*?

Maybe a part of me thought if she knew I was married she'd never want to see me again. Could that be the reason? Was I keeping my wife a secret so the daughter of my biggest client would keep having lunch with me?

My stomach lurched with guilt and I opened my mouth with the intention of telling her right there and then, honest to God I did, but I saw Mrs Holden approaching with a tray and the moment was lost.

'Thank you,' Lucy said as a ham sandwich was placed in front of her. I smiled my thanks.

Mrs Holden placed a teapot and two mismatched cups and saucers on the table and said, 'The tea'll need a minute or two,' before shuffling off again.

'I love this place,' Lucy said when we were alone again. She picked her sandwich up, 'I've never been anywhere like this before.' She took a bite and chewed.

'It's handy for work.'

'Tell me about your morning,' she said, putting the sandwich back on the plate and dabbing the corner of her mouth with her fingertip. 'What have you been doing?'

'Oh,' I said, trying not to show how happy I was that she was showing an interest in my life, 'nothing exciting.'

'You say that,' she said as she sort of looked me up and down in a very provocative manner, 'but it would be exciting to me. I have no idea what you do.'

'I can't really talk about it.' I put the strainer over her cup and poured tea into it, 'it's confidential.' If she had pressed me I think I would have told her every detail of the financial matters that I dealt with, but luckily for me she didn't.

She poured milk into her cup and looked at the spoon as she stirred. 'You're very good at keeping secrets, aren't you Daniel?'

I forced a smile to hide the nausea I was feeling.

'Your niece is a lovely girl.' Mrs Holden said as I approached the counter to settle the bill.

'Excuse me?' I thought I hadn't heard her right.

'Your niece,' Mrs Holden nodded towards Lucy who was standing by the door waiting for me, 'she's a lovely girl.'

'Yes, yes she is,' my fingers fumbled in my wallet as I struggled to find the money.

'Lovely manners,' she was counting the coins I had given her as she spoke.

'Yes, her mother brought her up properly.' I don't know why I offered that particular piece of information; my mouth was working independently of my brain.

'Your sister's girl is she?' She dropped the money into the drawer and closed it.

'Yes,' I said as I put my wallet back in my jacket, 'must rush or I'll be late back.' I headed for the door, thankful that Mrs Holden wouldn't know that I didn't have a sister.

'See you next week Mr Laither,' Mrs Holden said to my back, 'bye love.'

'You told her you were my niece?' The door had barely closed behind us before I asked the question.

'Yes,' she said, 'sorry. She asked me how I knew you and it was the first thing that came into my head.' I looked up and down the street which was deserted apart from two women coming out of the butchers. I turned back to Lucy and saw that she looked like she was going to cry. 'I'm sorry Daniel,' she said, 'please don't be mad at me.'

'I'm not mad at you,' I said, and I wasn't, not really. I was just sad that we had to involve yet another person in our deception. Too late now though, it was done and I... *we*... would have to deal with it.

'Shall I meet you for lunch on Monday?'

My instinct was to say no, we didn't need Mrs Holden asking any more questions. But I really did want to see her, if only to give her the gift I'd bought her.

LUCY

I knew that Daniel was meeting my father the day after our 'chance encounter' but the day after that I thought I'd go along to the café at lunch time and surprise him. Although we hadn't made an arrangement to meet I thought that he might expect me to be there, but I didn't mind that. What mattered was that he hoped that I would be there.

I could see as I walked past that he wasn't already there but the table he'd been sitting at the other day was free so I thought I'd go in and wait for him.

The woman behind the counter, the one that was always there, smiled at me when I went in. 'Hello love,' she said, 'nice to see you again.' I made a point of looking at the table in the corner, well, she's old and I thought she might need a hint. 'Oh don't worry, love,' she said. 'He'll be here. I've never known him to miss a Friday.'

That was music to my ears because I really didn't want to be in that greasy little café any longer than I needed to be. I smiled and sat down where I had the day before. The woman, I'm sorry I don't know her name, asked if she could get me anything while I waited so I ordered a pot of tea.

I looked around, willing Daniel to hurry up. I looked at my watch, it was almost twelve thirty so hopefully I wouldn't have long to wait.

'Friend of the family are you?' I had been lost in my own thoughts so I was surprised when the woman put the pot of tea on the table.

'He's my uncle,' I said. It was the first thing that came into my head. I couldn't tell her who I really was. Can you imagine what would have happened if I'd told her I was Daniel's lover? The poor woman would probably have had a heart attack. Actually I was quite impressed with how easily I'd come up with an answer. I should have been a spy.

She didn't contradict me when I said I was a family member so I thought it was safe to rule her out as Daniel's mother, which left me still wondering why he went there for his lunch. There were other, nicer places that he could go to eat.

The tea was disgusting but I pretended to sip it while I waited. As I looked out of the window I saw Daniel approaching, but he didn't see me until he was inside. His face lit up when he realised I was there but I noticed his eyes flitting around the room like he was checking if anyone had noticed.

He said he hadn't been expecting me, but I could tell that was a lie and it was obvious that he was pleased that I was there. The woman came over and we ordered ham sandwiches and a pot of tea for two. I'd barely touched the tea that she had brought me and when we were alone I said that I wanted to share the same pot as him. My God, you should have seen him blush.

It wasn't a hardship to be there with him, not really, other than we were in a grotty café and not a nice restaurant. I could tell that he liked me and that always makes me feel good. You show me a woman who doesn't like attention from men and I'll show you a liar. Every now and then I would catch him looking at me and then he would look away quickly once he realised that I'd noticed. It was like he couldn't believe that I was actually there. I don't suppose he ever thought in a million years that he would be sitting in that café having lunch with Lucy Braithwaite, not that I really class a couple of curled up ham sandwiches and a pot of stewed tea as lunch, but you know what I mean. I never actually asked him but he must have felt enormously flattered that I'd sought him out there. Flattered enough not to notice what was really happening.

After we'd eaten I waited at the door while he paid the bill. I saw him talking to the woman who worked there and when he came out he mentioned that I had told her I was his niece. At first he didn't seem very happy about it so I apologised and he forgave me in an instant. All I had to do was give him that look.

We agreed to meet the following week for lunch.

DANIEL

The following morning I sat on the edge of the bed with the bracelet in my hand and asked myself if I was really going to give it to Lucy. Was I really going to give a gift this extravagant to a woman who wasn't my wife?

I could hear Isobel moving around in the kitchen directly below where I was sitting. I could hear her clearing away the breakfast dishes. Maybe I should give the bracelet to her. She liked pretty things and the bracelet definitely fit that bill. Had I ever bought Isobel anything that pretty? I didn't think I had and I felt bad about that.

Just not bad enough to do the right thing and give it to her.

The third step from the bottom had a loose floor board so when I heard creaking on the stairs I knew that Isobel was on her way up. I quickly put the bracelet into the inside pocket of my jacket that was lying beside me on the bed and bent down to fiddle with my shoelaces.

'Is everything alright darling?' Isobel asked as she opened the door.

'Yes,' I said, pretending to fasten the shoelace that I had tied a good five minutes earlier. She started to make our bed by picking up my pillow and hitting it back into shape. I know it probably sounds mad but a little part of me wished that she would do that to my head. Maybe if I told her what I had done she would knock some sense into me.

Not that I had any real intention of telling her. Not then anyway, maybe not ever. How could I? It would hurt her so much, and that had never been my intention. I never wanted to hurt Isobel.

So why did I do it? Isn't that what you want to know? Well that makes two of us.

It's like I've tried to get you to understand, I was stuck in the middle of a terrible situation. On one hand Arthur Braithwaite had one of my bosses in some sort of head lock and he in turn had used me as a means of getting out of that position. On the other hand was Lucy. Lucy who showed me attention, who enjoyed being with me and who made me feel like a man.

But what sort of man was I? Certainly not the man I thought I was. The man I thought I was would never have betrayed his wife's trust.

Isobel shooed me off the bed so that she could straighten the sheets and I took that as my cue to leave. It was a bit earlier than I needed to leave but I made the excuse of having a lot of things to do. I was leaving earlier than I needed to more and more often.

I almost didn't go to the café. No, if I'm being honest, what I mean is, I thought about not going to the café. Isn't that what a dutiful husband would do? Wouldn't he stop it right there and then before it was too late? I wanted to be that dutiful husband and do the right thing, but I wanted to see Lucy more.

I went to the café just like I always knew I would. In fact I checked the clock every two minutes until it was time to go.

'I'm going to lunch,' I told Mrs Warren on the dot of twelve thirty.

'Right you are Mr Laither,' she said in the same way she did every day.

It was raining that day as I recall… Well, not rain as such but that drizzle, the sort that wets you to the bone without you really realising it. In some ways it was a good thing because it meant that I could run to the café and no-one gave me a second glance. Everyone was hurrying to get to wherever they were going.

I was almost at the door when I saw her running around the corner. She was wearing a cream coloured Mac and one of those rain hats, and neither seemed to be doing a good job of keeping her dry. We laughed as we almost bumped onto each other. Droplets of rain hung on to the ends of her eyelashes which made her eyes look like they were surrounded by tiny little diamonds. Tiny wrinkles appeared at the corners of her eyes as she smiled and I wanted to kiss her. I really wanted to kiss her.

But I knew that was impossible, so I opened the door and held it while she went inside.

'Come in out of the rain you two,' Mrs Holden said. 'You look like a pair of drowned rats.'

We took off our coats and hung them on the stand in the corner and as we did we shared furtive glances that sent a shiver through me from head to foot. Lucy used her fingers to put life back into the sections of her hair which had been flattened by her hat.

She was so beautiful.

We ordered some food and a pot of tea before taking what seemed to have become *our* seats. We both had our hands on the table and on a couple of occasions they even inched together before we drew them apart again.

There was no denying the connection between us. It was so strong. She was looking straight into my eyes and I couldn't have broken that link even if I had wanted to. I was helpless.

Eventually she patted the table and lowered her eyes with a coy smile on her face. I smiled too, though she didn't see that. I forced the smile off my lips as I caught a glimpse of Mrs Holden approaching us with a tray in her hands.

'You're becoming a regular,' Mrs Holden said to Lucy as she put a pot of tea on the table between us. 'Do you work round here?'

'Yes,' Lucy replied with barely any hesitation. 'I work in one of the offices on Musgrove Road.'

'One of the solicitors?' I thought she sounded sceptical.

Lucy sipped her tea to cover up the non-committal noise that she made.

'She asks a lot of questions, doesn't she?' Lucy whispered as soon as Mrs Holden was out of earshot.

Yes, she did, and I wondered if Mrs Holden hadn't been fooled by Lucy's niece story after all. There was just something about the questions she asked and the way she asked them that said to me that she didn't believe what she had been told.

Just like the day before we ate ham sandwiches and drank tea as we made small talk. She told me about what she had been doing since I had seen her the week before, but once again I was listening to the sound of her voice rather than the words that she spoke.

Just before it was time for me to go back to work, I took the bracelet from my jacket pocket and put it on the table between us.

'What's this?' she asked.

'I bought you a Christmas gift,' I pushed the box a couple of inches closer to her.

Her eyes were wide and excited like a child's as she said, 'I'd better keep this until Christmas morning, then.' She dropped the box into her bag that was sitting on the floor by her feet.

As I lay in bed on Christmas morning I wondered if she had opened her gift yet.

Isobel and I never had children, so it was just the two of us exchanging a gift or two by the fire in the living room after breakfast. She gave me a wallet and a scarf that she had knitted herself. I gave her the talcum powder and gloves. She seemed thrilled with them, especially the gloves. Her gratitude was like a knife in my chest.

I wondered if Lucy had felt the same way about her bracelet.

We had Christmas Dinner with Steven and Sylvia who are our oldest friends. Isobel has known Sylvia since God knows when and Steven and I were in the same class at grammar school. They don't have any children either so it made sense for us to share the festivities.

The meal was going to be a lavish affair compared to recent years which I know isn't that hard when you're comparing it to the war years and rationing, but when you're a childless couple food is what Christmas is about. I'd been looking forward to it ever since Sylvia had suggested it, and why wouldn't I? She was an excellent cook who had been able to work magic on the sparsest of ingredients, so I was eager to see what she could do with a real joint of meat. And then there was Stephen's homemade wine. I've had it before and it's not half bad. Just kidding, it's bloody awful, but it would have the desired effect. He'd given me a bottle for my birthday in October and I didn't remember anything after the second glass.

No, a day of feasting and friends sounded like just what the doctor ordered.

We'd been there an hour or so and the ladies were off in the kitchen working their magic when Stephen asked me if I was alright. I looked at him but couldn't find the right response. 'I'm just asking,' Stephen pressed, 'because you seem a bit...' He always chose his words carefully and finally settled on, 'distracted.'

'Do I?' I tried to laugh it off.

I tried telling him I was fine but I'm not sure he believed me. Why would he? He knew me better than anyone.

He was right of course, I had been distracted. I'd been thinking about Lucy, wondering what she as doing, wondering if she was wearing my bracelet. I couldn't tell any of that to Stephen though because he wouldn't understand. He wouldn't understand why what I had with Isobel wasn't enough for me. *I* didn't know why it wasn't enough for me. It had been enough for me until six short weeks before.

'I'm just tired,' I told him. I know it was the lamest of excuses but at least it wasn't a lie because I *was* tired. I hadn't slept properly in weeks. Something told me that Stephen didn't believe me any more than I believed myself.

At some point during the next couple of hours he told me that he had seen Big Don Francombe the week before. You'll not be surprised to hear that Big Don was so called because he was over six feet tall by the time he was twelve years old. He had been in our class at school but I hadn't seen him in years.

'How was he?' I asked. I was curious why Stephen had mentioned it, or rather the way he had mentioned it. There was something in his voice that made me think there was more to it than a throw away comment.

'I didn't speak to him because I don't think he saw me.' Stephen leaned forward in his armchair and gestured that I should do the same. He checked over his shoulder to check that no-one had come in without us realising it and then said in a stage whisper. 'He wasn't with his wife.'

'Oh?' My stomach hit the bottom of my throat.

'I saw him coming out of that little hotel on Paisley Avenue with a girl half his age.' His eyebrows lifted and he nodded his head.

My mouth was suddenly very dry and 'Oh?' was all I could manage.

'Yes,' he shifted even further towards me, 'and let me tell you, from the way that he was looking up and down the street he was somewhere that he shouldn't have been.' A tell-tale sign if ever there's been one. I knew that because I had done the same thing myself... more than once. 'We were at his wedding,' Stephen said, 'Marjorie is a lovely woman. I don't understand some men.' He threw his hands up in disbelief and sat back in his chair.

I thought of suggesting that there might have been a perfectly innocent reason for Big Don to be sneaking out of a hotel with a young woman in the middle of the afternoon but I thought the chance of that being the case was minimal, so I didn't bother. I shook my head instead in a non-committal sort of way.

'I mean,' Stephen was determined to address the point 'what possesses a man who has been married for what, ten, twelve years to do that sort of thing?'

I silently thanked God as Sylvia poked her head around the door and called us to the dinner table. It saved me feeling the need to defend someone that I saw as a kindred spirit.

We had been promised a feast and we weren't disappointed. As I sat at the table in my paper hat eating wonderful food and laughing with my nearest and dearest, I forgot for an hour or two at least just how complicated my life was becoming.

LUCY

Thank God that day was the last one that I ever had to go into that awful bloody café. I'd been trying to come up with a reason to stop going there and that busybody who worked there would finally give me one.

It was drizzling with rain and even though I'd only run about a hundred yards from where Robert had dropped me off my Mac was soaked by the time I got to the café. Daniel was running too, and we almost ran into each other. It was quite funny really.

My heart sank when Daniel ordered tea and sandwiches for us... again. I almost asked if the broth was available because that had at least been quite tasty whereas the sandwiches were horrible. Dry bread with next to no filling really isn't my idea of a sandwich. However, I had to pretend that they were the best things in the world and there was nothing else that I would rather eat.

As she brought our food she asked if I worked nearby and I told her that I did. What I really wanted to say was that it was none of her business but I didn't. I'd seen that as my opening, you see. Daniel had seemed uncomfortable when I had told her I was his niece and here I was telling her that I worked nearby, in a solicitor's office of all things. I could practically see Daniel squirm. I knew that he wouldn't take much persuasion to stop going there now and while I was eating those horrible sandwiches I was already dreaming of lovely restaurants with delicious food.

I was surprised when Daniel produced a box from his pocket and put it on the table.

It was a plain red box with no name on the top to give me a clue as to where it came from. I was pleased when he said that it was a Christmas present because that gave me the excuse to drop it in my bag and tell him that I would save it for Christmas Day.

Obviously I opened it that night.

It was a thin gold bracelet with tiny green stones dotted along its length. I say stones because there was no way they were a gem of any kind, let alone an emerald. They were just coloured glass. I wouldn't even be seen dead wearing it. I was so disappointed that Daniel would think for a second that I would wear anything like that. It was so cheap. Why would he think that I would wear coloured glass when I had real emeralds in my jewellery box?

I know I sound ungrateful but it really was just disappointment. I was happy that he had bought me a present; I just wished that it had been something better. It would be better next time; I would make sure of that.

This is the sort of thing I like. My father bought me this beautiful sapphire bracelet and I wear it almost all of the time now. Pretty, isn't it?

I put the bracelet Daniel had given me back in the box and dropped it in the bottom drawer of my dressing table. I assume it's still there because I never looked at it again.

DANIEL

Mrs Holden was placing my food on the table in front of me when she said, 'Not seen your niece in here for a bit. Not poorly is she?'

The comment caught me off guard so I had to think quickly. 'No,' I said, 'she's just changed jobs that's all.'

'Oh right, where's she working now?' Mrs Holden straightened my plate as she spoke.

'I'm not sure,' I said slowly, trying to give myself a second or two to think of something. 'Somewhere in Bristol,' and to this day I don't know why I said that.

As she shuffled away I realised that we had been right to stop meeting at the café on the corner for lunch. I wasn't sure that Mrs Holden actually suspected anything untoward but I knew that she asked too many questions for comfort and that couldn't be a good thing.

I told Lucy about it a couple of days later. 'Bristol?' she giggled. 'Why Bristol?'

'I don't know,' I laughed along with her, 'it was the first place that came into my head.'

We were lying together in the bed of room number seven at The Marsden. It had cost me ten bob to rent the room for one night and we would only be there for a little over an hour, but it was money well spent. That day in January was the fourth afternoon we had spent together that way.

That sounds terrible, doesn't it? What I just said about it being money well spent. I didn't mean it the way it sounded. I didn't mean it to sound like it wasn't a lot to pay for a bit of fun in the afternoon with someone before I went home to my wife. That's not what I meant at all. Anyway you could never describe Lucy Braithwaite as cheap.

That was the afternoon that I realised Lucy wasn't wearing the bracelet I bought her. I'd seen her maybe three of four times since Christmas and she hadn't even mentioned it. I know it probably wasn't up to her usual standard but I thought she might have worn it just once, especially when you consider the fuss she made when I didn't wear the watch she bought me. No, she wears this big sapphire thing that her father bought her instead. Mind, it probably cost more than my house so it's not hard to see why she would prefer it.

I knew that she was used to the better things in life. Since the day she was born she had had everything she ever wanted. Her father had seen to that. Maybe I would have been the same had I ever been lucky enough to have a daughter.

Not having a child used to be my biggest regret, but now with things the way they are, that's probably a good thing.

It was obvious by that stage that Lucy wanted more from our relationship than a couple of hours in a cheap hotel on the rare occasions that I could get away from work. She didn't seem to appreciate how hard it was for me to find those couple of hours away from the bank. Just that afternoon when I'd left the office I'd seen the look on Mrs Warren's face. She took care of my diary so she knew that I had nowhere that I needed to be. And now Lucy was talking about going to restaurants and to the theatre.

She was resting on her right elbow and using her left hand to stroke my chest as she said, 'Do you like the theatre Daniel?'

'I don't go much,' I said. The only time that Isobel and I had been to the theatre was before the war when we went to see a 'rep' production of that Shaw play, the one about the flower girl. Don't ask me what it was called because I don't know. It really wasn't my cup of tea but Isobel thought it was wonderful.

I really didn't fancy the idea of going to the theatre with Lucy. I couldn't see her sitting through a 'rep' production of anything; she probably went to London whenever she wanted to see a show and I didn't think I could stretch to that.

'I love the theatre,' she said thoughtfully. She held her bottom lip between her teeth as she ran her fingernail down my breast bone. 'Did you enjoy the lunch at Poplar Lodge?' she asked.

'Of course I did,' I admitted.

'I love nice restaurants,' the sentence hung between us. She started to kiss me again, giving me tiny little pecks on the lips between words. 'Much as I enjoy these afternoons together, I would like to go out sometimes.'

I noticed that her eyes had flicked to the side briefly and when I checked I saw that they had looked at the dressing table. Its paint was chipped and there were dark stains around the edge of the mirror. Not the sort of place that Lucy was used to.

'That would be nice,' I said but I'm not sure I meant it.

She kissed me again, harder this time.

I watched Lucy as she dressed. She lingered over rolling her stockings up and I knew that it was for my benefit, you know, to tease me. She liked to tease me. I couldn't imagine not seeing her, not being with her, and I accepted that if I was going to carry on seeing her I was going to have to up my game. Obviously sex in the afternoon in a hotel that was little better than a flea-pit wasn't enough for her anymore and I didn't blame her. Having said that, even though I knew that I really did want to carry on seeing Lucy, would I have dared to stop? Remember how she'd made a point of telling me that her father didn't like it when she was unhappy. I don't know if she'd meant it as a threat but that was the way I'd taken it. Arthur Braithwaite could make my life very difficult is he chose to and I didn't much fancy that. Anyway, I was enjoying his daughter too much. But I knew that I was going to have to try harder to keep her happy.

Lucy was used to the best things in life. She was used to fine dining and yet she had gone to Mrs Holden's café just to spend time with me, and I don't suppose she had ever spent time in a hotel like The Marsden before. She had lowered her standards and I realised that if I wanted to keep seeing her I would have to raise my own. She deserved to be treated in the way that she was used to.

I needed a plan and I quickly came up with one.

Before we left the room I asked her if she would go out to dinner with me. I told her it wouldn't be Poplar Lodge but it would be somewhere nice. They all knew her at Poplar Lodge, and some of them had seen me there, too. The last thing I needed was someone seeing us there together and casually dropping it into conversation with her father. That was the excuse I gave anyway. The truth is that I would probably have to use Isobel's housekeeping money for the month to pay for a meal there.

Her face lit up at the suggestion and she said, 'I'd like that very much Daniel.'

In the cold light of day I realised that I'd been a bit rash saying that we would go somewhere nice for dinner. I know I earned a decent salary but at the end of the day I was still just a bank manager with a mortgage to service and a wife who expected regular housekeeping.

Besides, my idea of a nice restaurant might not be the same as Lucy's. I don't suppose she's ever had to worry about how much a meal will cost, but I have, and I was wondering how I was going to pay for this one.

In the end I decided that I'd give the savings a miss for once. I've put money into what Isobel likes to call the 'Chestnut Avenue Fund' regularly for a couple of years, but that month the money would go to what I decided to call the 'Make Lucy Happy Fund.'

Have you ever been to that restaurant near the Town Hall? Well, I always thought it looked the part and I took a quick look at the menu the following morning as I walked past on my way to work. Pricey, but I thought I could manage it. There was a telephone number at the top of the menu which, as luck would have it, I was able to memorise because it was only a couple of digits different to the bank's.

I made the reservation that day at lunchtime. I rang from a public phone box and used an assumed name. I used the name Patterson

It was the best part of a week before I saw Lucy again. It was a nice crisp January day and she suggested that we go for a walk in the park. I've got to be honest, it wasn't how I'd hoped we'd spend the afternoon, but on the bright side I saved ten bob that I could put towards our dinner date.

I told her about the restaurant I'd booked as we walked along. She smiled at me and said, 'That will be lovely Daniel, thank you.'

My hands were in the pockets of my overcoat and she linked her arm through mine. She seemed happy

I was glad that Lucy was happy because by that point I think I had actually started to feel something for her, something bordering on love.

The night that I'd told Lucy about the reservation I'd sat opposite Isobel at the dining table and felt terrible. In all

116

the years we had been married I had never taken my wife to a posh restaurant.

'I'm sorry Isobel,' I said as I pushed cabbage around the plate, 'but I have to go out next Thursday evening.'

'Oh.' She looked up from her food.

'Yes, I have to have dinner with a client.' I hated lying to her but I justified it by thinking that it was almost the truth. I did occasionally have dinner with clients, so she accepted it readily.

Before I left work that Thursday, the first time I actually took Lucy out anywhere, I made sure that I withdrew plenty of cash. I hoped it would be enough because I really didn't want to pay for dinner by cheque. Isobel rarely, if ever, looked at bank statements – I mean who better to look after your family finances than a bank manager? – but better to be safe than sorry. Like I said, she didn't usually look at statements but I didn't want to have to start hiding them away in case that made her suspicious.

I'd spent the best part of the day imagining how the evening would go, a process that left me with a feeling in my stomach that I couldn't really identify – something between nausea and excitement.

When I got home, instead of changing my clothes and settling down to an evening by the fire with my wife, I washed and shaved before putting on my best suit and preparing to meet Lucy.

Before I left the bedroom, I found the coat that I kept in the back of the wardrobe and took the watch that Lucy had

117

bought me out of the inside pocket where I had kept it hidden since the day she had given it to me. I'd told her it was a watch for special occasions and I thought this would count as one.

I wrapped it in my handkerchief and put it in my trouser pocket before straightening my tie and, after checking myself in the mirror one last time, I turned off the light and left the bedroom.

Isobel was waiting for me at the bottom of the stairs. She was holding my overcoat in her hands and after she had helped me into it she brushed her hands across the shoulders to flatten them.

'Will you be late?' she asked.

'Shouldn't think so,' I said, trying to sound casual, 'but I'll take a key so go to bed if you're tired.'

The door to the living room was open and as I glanced through it I saw a tray sitting on the coffee table. A sandwich and a cup of tea were on it.

'Is that all you're having?' I asked.

She smiled as she said that it was. She said that she would be fine. I'd have to be a total prick not to feel guilty about her eating a ham sandwich while I was spending the best part of a week's wages on a meal to share with Lucy. And for what it's worth I did feel guilty. I felt sick about it. Just not enough to not go.

'Have a good time,' she said before kissing my cheek, 'hopefully it won't be shop talk all evening.'

I tried to smile back.

As I walked away from her and felt her eyes on my back, bile stung the back of my throat.

Isobel didn't deserve what I was doing to her but I couldn't stop myself.

You'll say that I could have stopped myself if I'd really wanted to, and you're right. I didn't want to hurt Isobel but I didn't want to stop seeing Lucy either. What can I say; I am a weak and selfish man.

Once I was out of sight I took the watch out of my pocket and secured in into place on my wrist.

We had arranged to meet outside the library but she was late and I started to wonder if she would turn up. As I hopped from foot to foot, looking up and down the street, I had a feeling that I'd forgotten my wallet, and although I knew that I'd put it in the inside pocket of my jacket I had to check, just in case. It'd be bloody embarrassing if I couldn't pay for the meal after we'd eaten it. As I opened my coat and tapped my wallet I heard the clip clop of heels on the pavement and I turned my face towards the sound.

It was Lucy.

She looked stunning. There was a full moon that night which created a sort of haze around her, lighting her up. Her pale green coat was fastened all the way up to her neck to keep the cold out and her pearl drop earrings brushed her collar. She looked like she had made an effort and, alright I'll be honest, I was flattered that she had made that effort just for me.

If I close my eyes I can see her standing there as clear as day, except it was night but you know what I mean. I'm ashamed to say that I couldn't tell you what Isobel had been wearing that night. I don't think I could even tell you what she was wearing the last time I saw her.

But Lucy looked gorgeous that night and she was there to see me.

'Hello Daniel,' she said coyly, 'I'm sorry I'm late. I couldn't decide what to wear.' She reached up and kissed my cheek. 'You haven't been waiting long, have you?'

'No,' I lied.

We walked to the restaurant arm in arm.

The restaurant was called Scarlet, and although it wasn't full, there were plenty of people sat at tables when we got there. It hadn't been open long and I guess a lot of people were trying it out. Lucy said that it had had a good review in the local paper.

When we got there a woman came forward to take our coats. She helped Lucy out of her coat and it took everything I had to keep my jaw from hitting the floor. The dress she was wearing showed her figure off to perfection. I knew I blushed when she caught me looking at her but I couldn't drag my eyes away.

A man approached us and asked if we had a reservation. I said we did and when he asked what the name was and as I said Patterson I heard Lucy give a little giggle. She tried to dismiss it as a sneeze, but I knew it wasn't.

He lowered not only his head but his eyes which more or less told me that he didn't believe me, but what did I care? Chances were I was never going to see him again after that night so what did it matter? He did look at Lucy a second or two longer than I thought was necessary though, but she did look gorgeous and he was a man, so who was I to blame him?

None of the other diners paid me any attention as we were led to our table, but a couple of the men gave Lucy a second glance. And she was with me. Can you imagine how good that made me feel?

The food was delicious and at those prices it had to be. It cost me more than half a week's wages but it was worth it just to see Lucy smiling at me across the table. There was only one disappointment for me that night, and that was that she wasn't wearing the bracelet I'd bought her. I'd made a point of wearing her watch. I didn't want it to spoil the evening, so I tried to push it to the back of my mind. I managed it at the time, but when I think about it now it really pisses me off because I have never seen her wear it.

After we'd left the restaurant she used the phone box outside the library to ring Robert, that bald headed bloke who works for her father. She rang him to come and pick her up and he said he'd be there in ten minutes. That gave us five minutes to stand together hand in hand before I had to kiss her goodnight. She'd had a gin and orange and I could taste it on her lips.

I didn't like the idea of leaving her alone, even for just a few minutes, so after that goodnight kiss I moved into the shadows of the building where I could see her without anyone seeing me.

'I had a lovely evening Lucy,' I said, though I don't think she heard me.

I was tempted to go to her and put my arms around her but I saw a car coming around the corner and true to his word Robert was there ten minutes after she had called him. He got out of the car and walked around to open the door for her. I watched him looking at her and realised that he was in love with her too.

LUCY

We were in bed at The Marsden when Daniel told me that he had told the woman in the café that I had moved to Bristol. I hadn't been there for over a week and apparently she had asked if I was ill. I realised that she couldn't have cared less if I was ill or not, she was just being nosey, but Daniel seemed to think that she was just being kind. I wanted to tell him to stop being so naïve but I thought better of it. I was just glad that I wouldn't have to go there again.

That was when I thought I'd chance my arm and suggest that we should stop going to The Marsden as well. It is literally a flea-pit and I've had the bites to prove it. It's ten shillings a night for goodness sake! So what does that tell you? It's a dump. I'd been willing to put up with it at the start just to snare Daniel but now that I had him, well, he was going to have to pay for the privilege.

He didn't take much persuading, just the right look, a kiss, and a well-placed touch. 'I love the theatre,' I told him, 'don't you love the theatre?' I don't actually care for it at all but I just had to sow the right seed. I prefer nice restaurants.

It worked, of course, and before we left the room that day he had asked me if I would like to go to dinner with him. The silly thing is that he made it sound like it had been completely his own idea.

He said that Poplar Lodge was out of the question because the staff there knew me and some of them would know him. He implied that it wouldn't be a good idea for one of them to tell my father that we had been there together. I knew the real reason was that he couldn't afford it but I let him think what he liked because I didn't want to bruise his ego.

Not to worry, as long as he took me somewhere. It was vital that we were seen out in public... and before you say that we were seen out together in that café, nobody who matters would go there so that didn't count.

We'd sort of fell into the routine of meeting once a week and that suited me fine because that gave me time for Thomas. Do you know Thomas Wentworth? His father is very rich. He's another one that doesn't like his name shortening. Anyway, I'd sort of started seeing Thomas around Christmas time so I spent most of my time with him. The Thursday afternoons that I spent with Daniel didn't interfere with anything that I would do with Thomas.

I knew that I would have to come up with a reason why I couldn't see him on a Thursday evening but that wouldn't be a problem.

I'm sure you're wondering why I only saw Daniel once a week. Think about it. Daniel had another life, his real life, one in which he and I weren't so much as having a cup of tea together let alone rampant sex. Sorry to go on about it but it really was what the relationship was based on. Anyway I thought that even Daniel could find an excuse for getting away once a week and I didn't want to make things difficult for him. Not at that point anyway, that would come later. It gave me the best of both worlds in many respects. I had Daniel and the delights he had to offer me, and Thomas who wined and dined me. He wasn't as good as Daniel in the bed department but his wallet more than made up for that.

So it was the following Thursday afternoon that Daniel said he was going to make reservations at Scarlet, you know that place near the Town Hall. It had had some good reviews in the local papers and I just hoped that he'd be able to afford it. It'd be so embarrassing if he couldn't. I didn't feel bad about it though because he'd hardly spent a lot on me before then, had he? He'd booked a room in a hotel a few times and bought me a couple of meals in that café but that was all. I didn't even count the bracelet because to be honest I've had better things out of a Christmas cracker. No, it was about time he spent a bit of money on me.

I'd told my father about Daniel's plan and he seemed to approve. Obviously I kept my mother in the dark because she and Thomas' mother are friends and the last thing I needed was Margot Wentworth finding out that I was two-timing her son. And rest assured my mother would have told her. She would do anything to get one over on me. So when she asked me why I wasn't seeing Thomas that Thursday night and where I was going I told her that I was seeing my friend Elizabeth.

'Bit dressed up for seeing Elizabeth, aren't you?' she sneered.

'There's nothing wrong with wanting to look nice,' I said.

She shrugged her shoulders and went back to the magazine she had been flicking through. I went out to the car where Robert was waiting to drive me into town.

I'd arranged to meet Daniel outside the library and he was already there when the car turned into the street. I knew he would be because I'd deliberately arrived a little bit late… well, it's good to keep a man guessing.

I asked Robert to drop me a bit further along near the church and I waited until the car was out of sight before I walked the short distance back to where Daniel was waiting for me.

'Hello,' he said when he finally saw me. He looked really nervous but a big smile spread over his face as I walked up to him.

'Hello.' I whispered.

I said I was sorry for being late though I can't remember what excuse I gave. He said it didn't matter.

'You look lovely,' he said and he was right, I did. I'd chosen my dress carefully and taken care with my make-up. He couldn't see my dress at that point of course, but I knew he'd be impressed once he did see it. It was pale green chiffon and fitted everywhere that it should.

'So do you.' I said giving him the once over. It's true; he did look nice or rather he would once he got his overcoat off. His coat, which had seen its best days years ago, was open despite the cool January evening and I could see his suit underneath it. The suit was charcoal grey which he wore with a white shirt and a pale blue tie. I thought it was probably his best suit, the one he kept for special occasions like weddings. One of John Collier's finest fifty shillings suits. I'm sorry I shouldn't mock because they really are decent for what they are but there's just no comparison between them and the suits that my father has made to measure.

I don't suppose you care about what he was wearing, do you?

'Shall we?' he said as he offered me his arm. We walked together, arm in arm, the short distance to the restaurant and it actually felt quite romantic.

Like the gentleman he is, Daniel held the door open for me. There was a woman sitting to one side ready to take our coats. This was the moment I'd been waiting for. I opened the coat slowly and allowed it to slip off my shoulders into the woman's hands.

Oh my goodness, you should have seen Daniel's face. I thought his eyes were going to pop out of his head. He couldn't take his eyes off me.

A man in a suit had appeared from somewhere and approached us. 'Good evening sir,' he said, 'do you and the young lady have a reservation this evening?'

'Yes,' I felt Daniel's hand on the base of my spine.

'And the name please?' he spoke so beautifully.

'Patterson,' Daniel said, 'Mr Patterson.'

Well at least it wasn't Smith.

The man consulted the book and then said, 'This way please.'

He looked at me longer than he needed to and for a second I feared that he might have recognised me. Not as Lucy Braithwaite as such, but as someone who had been there the week before with someone else. Thomas and I had been there the previous Friday, you see. The old lech had looked at me too long that time as well.

The restaurant wasn't full, but there were people already there and a few of them looked at us as we were lead to our table.

I ordered the haddock and Daniel had chicken and we both had trifle for dessert. We shared a bottle of white wine and after coffee we each had a night cap. I discovered that Daniel was a whiskey drinker which he took with just a splash of water. I smiled to myself when he ordered it because that's exactly what my father would have ordered. I had a gin and orange. I watched him when the bill was placed in front of him and I think I saw his colour drain a little bit. His hands were shaking as he counted the notes out and he left a two shilling tip.

If you were to ask me now what we talked about I wouldn't be able to tell you. I don't think we talked about much really, we never did. It wasn't that sort of relationship.

When we left the restaurant we walked back to the library where I used the public telephone to ring Robert and ask him to come and get me. He said he'd be there in ten minutes.

For the first five minutes Daniel and I stood close together huddling up against the frost that was starting to form and then he kissed me very gently on the lips, thanked me for a lovely evening and disappeared into the shadows. I couldn't see him but I could sense him watching me, making sure that I was safe until Robert arrived. At one point I heard him mumble something though for the life of me I don't know what it was.

Just before I got into the car I smiled at where I thought he was. He'd earned it

DANIEL

For the first five minutes Daniel and I stood close together huddling up against the frost that was forming and then he kissed me very gently on the lips, thanked me for a lovely evening and disappeared into the shadows.

What I've told you before has been bringing us to this point because the real trouble started after that night at Scarlet.

You see, now that we'd been out properly in public there was no going back. Spending a little time in a cheap hotel was no longer enough for Lucy. As far as she was concerned we were a couple now and couples went out together. I'm sure you'll have guessed that Lucy always got what she wanted, though I couldn't for the life of me guess why she wanted me. Obviously I was flattered, I've said that before, but when I really thought about it, when I was alone in the middle of the night, I couldn't understand what she saw in me. I'm not putting myself down here, I'm not saying I'm ugly or anything but I know what I am and I am not the sort of bloke that the likes of Lucy Braithwaite would go for.

And remember, she was the one that came after me. Sometimes it just didn't make sense.

But sensible or not we were in a relationship and I wasn't prepared to give it up. I wasn't prepared to give her up.

But we weren't playing the same game anymore, I realised that, and somehow I was going to have learn a whole new set of rules.

And it all cost money, money that I didn't have, or at least didn't have spare.

130

I'd always been careful with money – it comes with the territory I suppose – and I had a little of it put away but that was meant to go towards the house that Isobel wanted on Chestnut Avenue. Even if we sold the house we were in for the full market value we would still need a sizeable mortgage to buy even the smallest house on that road so every spare penny we had was going towards that.

I couldn't take more of that money... could I? That house was the reason that I had allowed myself to get involved in this mess in the first place. The promotion that William Morris had implied would be mine would come with a decent pay rise; one that would take us closer to achieving our dream. It had always been more her dream than mine, but she was right about a new house. It would look better for my standing within the community.

How could I possibly use the money that was supposed to be going towards our new house on another woman?

Quite easily as it turned out because, like I said a while ago, I was selfish. I never wanted Isobel to get hurt, though how I thought that was avoidable I don't know. I wasn't thinking straight and I hadn't been thinking straight since before Christmas.

It was the beginning of March when I told Isobel that I had joined a Gentleman's Club. She didn't seem to mind, in fact she even said that it would probably be good for my career, and she described it as 'A good place to make connections.' I took to going to 'my club' on a Thursday evening where I ate with my fellow club members, had a few drinks and talked business. God love her she seemed pleased for me.

Of course there was no Gentleman's Club, there was only Lucy. We would meet for an early dinner and take it from there. Sometimes we would go to the pictures or other times just go for a walk. The weather was getting better by then. Occasionally we went to a hotel for a couple of hours, but not every time. We'd moved on from The Marsden and gone up market. To me a bed was a bed, it wasn't like we would be spending much time there, but Lucy had her standards.

'I wish we didn't have to do this,' Lucy said one Thursday night as we were getting dressed.

'Do what?' I couldn't believe that she was suggesting we gave up the physical side of our relationship. Turned out she wasn't.

'Get out of bed, get dressed and go home.' She pulled a face the way that a child would.

'We have to go home,' I said but she looked at me with those big eyes of hers and before I knew what I was doing I'd said, 'Let's go way for the night.'

The smile returned to her face and she was happy again.

I spent the next few days wondering what the hell I'd let myself in for. How was I supposed to get away for a night? Do you think Isobel would have believed me if I'd told her that my club was having a trip to the sea-side? No? I didn't either which is why I didn't say it.

You see the trouble with Isobel is that she was too trusting.

When I'd told her that I had to have dinner with a client she straightened my coat so that I would look nice. When I'd told her that I was joining a Gentleman's Club she thought it was a good career move. So when I told her that I was going to a work meeting which involved an overnight stay, she believed me. It was the only thing that I could come up with.

She even congratulated me, said that my name must be being mentioned in the right places if I was being invited to regional meetings. Why didn't she think about it? The bank only has branches in this county and you can get to anywhere in this county within two hours. Why would I need to stay away? I sometimes wonder if she knew that I was having an affair and chose to ignore it.

Maybe she's partly to blame.

LUCY

At last Daniel started taking me places other than The
Marsden, and I thanked God for that. If I'd had to spend
one more minute in that bloody hotel I might have told my
father that he needed someone else to deal with Daniel. It
wasn't what went on in the hotels that I minded, just that
particular dive.

We'd had the lovely dinner at Scarlet and after that
success he said that we should do it more often. I agreed
with him. I have no idea what excuse he used to get out of
the house, mainly because I didn't want to know, but we
started meeting every Thursday evening. We usually had
dinner somewhere and we even went to the pictures once or
twice. Now and again we would go to a hotel for an hour or
so. The restaurants were always decent ones and now the
hotels were too, so I don't know how much it was costing
him or where he was getting the money from. That's the
good thing about being a lady though, isn't it? It's the
man's job to worry about money.

Then one Thursday night around Easter time we went to
a hotel for a bit of fun after dinner and as we were getting
dressed I said something about wishing that we didn't have
to go. I said that I wished we could spend the night together,
the whole night. I thought I might be pushing my luck but
you know what they say about nothing ventured nothing
gained. I was putting the idea in his head. I mean he'd just

had a taster of what he could have if we spent the night together.

At first he just said that we couldn't, he said that we had to go home, but all it took was that face, the one that I always use when I want something. You know the one, down-turned mouth and wide eyes. I call it my sad face, though I've never once used it when I actually have been sad. All I had to do was pull that face and the next thing I know; he's suggesting that we go somewhere overnight.

had a taster of what he could have if we spent the night together.

At first he just said that we couldn't, he said that we had to go home, but after all it took was that face, the one that I

DANIEL

I booked a B&B for the last Wednesday in April. It was near the old castle, so out of town, in a nice bit of countryside. I remember Johnson and his wife going there for their honeymoon a couple of years ago and he'd said how nice it was. That might have had more to do with being a newly wed than the surroundings but he'd said it was romantic, so that would do for me.

Once again I gave my name as Patterson. I used it whenever I made a reservation for me and Lucy.

It may only have been about ten miles away from the centre of town but I was still going to need to get us there. Walking was out of the question and I think we can both guess what Lucy's answer would have been if I'd suggested the bus.

Isobel must have been thinking about the same problem but obviously with a different destination in mind.

'How are you getting there?' she asked in all innocence as we ate our supper one evening. 'It must be forty miles to Head Office. Couldn't you get a lift with someone?'

'No,' I said. By then I found that lying to my wife was becoming much easier. 'No-one else I know is going.'

'Well what about what's-his-name?' she asked. 'Williams? The one from the High Street branch. Is he not going?'

'As far as I can tell it's only certain sub branches.' The lie tripped so easily off my tongue. 'As far as I can make out I'm the only one from town going.'

'Why don't you ask Stephen if you can borrow his car?' She carried on nibbling at her food, totally unaware that she might have come up with the answer. After she swallowed her food, put her knife and fork down and dabbed the corner of her mouth with her napkin she said, 'We really should think of getting a car of our own. I mean I know we can manage at the moment but when we move to Chestnut Avenue we're going to need a car. I'll bet you're the only bank manager in town that catches the bus to work,' she laughed as she started eating her food again.

Would she ever let up about Chestnut Avenue? No, of course she wouldn't. We'd discussed it; we'd decided that it was what we wanted. Now she wanted a car too. However, the more I thought about that the more I liked it. A car would make seeing Lucy easier. At the minute we were meeting somewhere in town and either walking or getting a taxi to wherever we were going, a car of my own would solve all that. It wouldn't have to be anything fancy, it would just need to be decent. Lucy wouldn't go anywhere near an old banger. Maybe I could get a loan to cover the cost.

'So what do you think?'

It took me a second or two realise that Isobel was talking again.

'I think you're right,' I said, 'I'm sure Stephen can manage without the car for one night. I'll talk to him tomorrow.'

Later on that evening I kissed her and called her a clever girl for coming up with such good idea and after I'd done it I hated myself a little bit more.

'Sorry, no can do,' Stephen said the following day.

'Why not?' I don't think I hid my disappointment very well. 'Couldn't you walk to work for one day?'

'Nothing to do with that Daniel,' he said as I put the pint of beer I'd just bought down on the table he was sitting at.

'Well why then?' I asked as I took a sip from my own pint.

I had to wait until he'd finished his first sip and licked the froth from his upper lip before he answered. 'Don't you watch the news?'

And that was when the penny dropped and what I thought was my perfect plan started to fall apart at the seams. 'Of course, I didn't think.'

'Why would you? You're not trying to get by on two hundred miles worth of petrol a month are you? I thought we'd done away with rationing. I haven't got that sort of allowance left, not after going to see Sylvia's mother in hospital. That was a sixty mile round trip. Six bob a gallon I paid last week, six bob. I never thought I'd see the day. There'll be no cars left on the road before long if they don't sort out that mess in Suez.'

He spent the next ten minutes going on about the state of the country and the world in general. What had he fought in the war for? Blah, blah, blah. I know he's my best friend but he doesn't half go on sometimes, and over the years I've learned to switch off. Anyway I had more important things to worry about, like how I was going to get Lucy to the aptly named Paradise View hotel.

'Sorry I can't help you,' I heard him say, 'but you can see how I'm fixed. With Sylvia's mum being the way she is we have to save every mile we can.'

'It's alright Stephen,' I said, 'I understand. How does it look for Sylvia's mum?' Showing an interest seemed like the decent thing to do.

He looked at me grimly and shook his head. 'We're just waiting for the phone call. It's just a matter of time.'

'I'm sorry to hear that,' I said, and I was.

We drank in silence for a couple of minutes, each of us considering our own predicaments I suppose, or at least I was.

'What did you need it for anyway?' Stephen asked.

'Work thing.' I said vaguely.

He gave me a look that said he was surprised to hear what I had just said. Although we didn't work together we spoke about work a lot and he knew fine well that me having nights away from home for work were as rare as hen's teeth. 'Unusual.' I couldn't help but feel that he was calling me out in a lie which disappointed me almost as much as him telling me I couldn't borrow his car.

'I know,' well it was unusual so why deny it, 'I don't know what it's all about. It's all a bit hush hush.'

'What? You mean that surly bugger that runs the High Street branch doesn't know? I thought he knew everything. You should see the way he parades about that place telling everyone what to do.' He was laughing as he spoke.

'He's not going.' I realised how ridiculous it sounded.

'Is he not? In that case I might have a bit of fun with him next time I'm in.' Stephen said between sips of beer. 'Let him know that there are things going on at Head Office that he doesn't know about. What day did you say you were going?'

'You'd best not,' I said. 'Whatever it is, like I said it's pretty hush hush so you'd better keep it to yourself.' I am fully aware of how pathetic that sounded but the last thing I needed was Stephen mentioning anything to anyone at the High Street branch. 'I don't understand why you still go there anyway,' I said desperately trying to change the subject. 'You should get your account transferred over to my branch.'

'It's handy for work,' he said as he drained his glass, 'fancy another?'

'Go on then,' I said. 'I don't suppose they're expecting us back yet anyway.'

'What will you do?' Isobel asked me when I told her what Stephen had said.

'I don't know.'

In the end, it was Lucy who came to the rescue... or rather her friend did.

We met as usual on the Thursday before we were due to go to the B&B and the first thing she said was that she had something to tell me. She kept me waiting until we had ordered dessert though. We were in that little Italian at the bottom of the high street, you know, the one that's owned by the man who says he comes from Naples. She'd been dying to tell me all night, and in the end she got to it.

'It's about next Wednesday,' she said.

LUCY

'Where are you going?' Thomas asked me. 'You usually see me on a Wednesday.'

We were having dinner together at Poplar Lodge and I'd waited until after the main course to tell him.

'Yes, well, I'm sorry but this time I can't.' Thomas really was getting a bit too possessive and I didn't like that.

'But the show has come up from the West End and it's only here for one night,' he said. 'Can't you make your girls night away some other time?'

'It won't be Josie's birthday any other time will it, silly,' I said. I lowered my head and looked up at him. He seemed to like it and I used that look a lot. He would forgive me anything after that look.

'Well it's just bloody inconvenient of her to have her birthday on that Wednesday,' he said with a fake pout and we both laughed. 'So where are you going?'

'To stay with her grandmother,' I said. 'Apparently they share the same birthday.'

'Where does she live?' He asked as a hand appeared at the side of me delivering my customary crème brûlée.

If I'd told the truth I would have said the cemetery. Instead I said, 'In the country.'

'How are you getting there?' He sat back as a different hand put his dessert on the table.

'I don't know.' I said as I tapped the hard topping. That was my favourite bit and I was starting to wish he'd shut up.

However, I forgot all about the crisp sugar when he said. 'Take my car.'

'What?' I could hardly believe my ears.

'Take my car,' he reached across the table and took my hands and for the first time ever I didn't want to snatch them away. 'You can drive, can't you?'

'Of course.' I laughed. I can, I just don't often have to.

I let him squeeze my hands. 'Then I insist you drive Julie...'

'Josie.' I couldn't stop myself correcting him. It's important when you're lying to keep the story accurate all of the time.

He didn't seem to mind, '...Josie to her grandmother's in style.'

I felt like kissing him but somehow managed to stop myself just in time.

DANIEL

Why didn't Isobel see what was happening right in front of her face? Aren't women supposed to have a sixth sense about things?

If she had only said to me then that she suspected something I think I would have come clean and thrown myself on her mercy. But she didn't do that. No, she fussed over me and made sure that my shirt was ironed properly so that I would 'look the part' in front of the bosses. She made sure that my razor was packed and she even cleaned my shoes for God's sake. What was wrong with her?

Always the perfect wife, that's Isobel. Perfectly clean house, perfectly cooked food, perfect bloody wife.

I'm sorry I shouldn't say that about her. Before all this happened I loved my perfectly clean house and my perfectly cooked meals. What man wouldn't? I'll never know why it wasn't enough for me.

But it wasn't and I left her that Wednesday morning with a customary kiss on the cheek and an overnight bag in my hand.

I'd told her that one of the managers from one of the other sub branches had been called to the meeting at the last minute and that we were going together. I'd had to come up with something because when I'd told her that I couldn't borrow Stephen's car the only alternative would be for me to go there by train. I'd thought that was a

144

perfectly good option until she decided that she would come and see me off at the station.

I didn't go to work that day. I caught the bus as usual but got off a couple of stops early and went to the train station instead. A man with an overnight bag doesn't look out of place at a train station does he?

I found a telephone box as far away from the platform as I could find and prayed that a train didn't come through in the few minutes that it would take me to ring work.

I huddled over the telephone receiver and waited for Mrs Warren to pick her end up.

'Good morning, Mr Laither's office,' she said with her usual efficiency.

I attempted to make my voice as deep and nasal as I could. 'Good morning Mrs Warren.'

'Mr Laither?' She made my name sound like a question.

'Yes,' I added a little cough in at that point for good measure. 'I'm just ringing to say that I won't be in today. I've woken up with a terrible head cold.'

'You need some honey and lemon for that,' she said, 'maybe even a drop of whiskey too if you've got any left from Christmas.'

'I'll bear that in mind,' I said, 'but right now I'm going to go back to bed to try and sleep it off.'

'Best thing for you.' I imagined her nodding her head the way that she usually did when she was agreeing with me. 'Shall I ask Mr Bridge to take your appointments?'

I'd made a point the day before of making detailed preparations for what I had in my diary for the rest of the week. I was taking a risk letting Bridge take my meetings especially when he was going to be so well prepared. It was a risk I was willing to take. 'If you wouldn't mind,' I said, throwing another cough in, 'thank you very much.'

'I hope you're feeling better soon Mr Laither,' she sounded genuinely concerned and I felt bad about deceiving her.

'I'm sure it's nothing to worry about,' I said, 'a couple of days in bed should see me right as rain. I expect I'll be back in on Friday.'

'Right you are then Mr Laither, you just concentrate on getting better. Tell Mrs Laither I said hello.'

The phone went dead as I said, 'Thank you, I will.'

I spent the next three hours sitting in the canteen drinking lukewarm tea and reading a newspaper that I had bought from the stand beside the ticket office. There's nothing suspicious about a man with an overnight bag sitting in a station canteen drinking tea. Lucky for me there was a shift change after I'd been there about an hour and the old lady who had obviously opened the place up early in the morning was replaced by a younger woman who was only interested in the porter who was leaning on the counter. She'd occasionally ask him if he had no work to do but apparently he didn't and he was still propping up the counter watching the woman when I left.

I had agreed to meet Lucy by the main entrance to the park at one o'clock. For all it's the main entrance, it's down a side street and there was very little chance of us being spotted.

146

I got there with ten minutes to spare and I wished she would hurry up because a man with an overnight bag does look out of place outside a park entrance.

I saw the nose of a Bentley inching its way around the corner. It's not a car built for back streets and its driver seemed to be having a bit of trouble navigating around the tight bend. I got the shock of my life to see Lucy at the wheel. When she'd said that she was borrowing a friend's car I hadn't expected anything like that. It was a magnificent car and I could hardly believe that I was actually going to ride in it.

As I watched the car inch towards me, I realised for the first time that I might not be the only man in Lucy's life. That Bentley may have belonged to her 'friend' but I was willing to bet my life that her 'friend' was a man. Beautiful as it was, no woman would choose to drive that car. No, this car belonged to a man, a rich man. And not just a rich man, a rich man that Lucy was seeing, possibly sleeping with. You wouldn't just lend that car to just anyone, though you might lend it to your lover. It appeared to me that I wasn't the only one being unfaithful and that thrilled me more than I can say.

Was I jealous? Of course I bloody was. I was taking her to a three quid a night B&B and her other bloke drove a Bentley. How could I compete with that? I didn't know but clearly I was doing something right because she was going away with me. I was her 'bit on the side' but I thought that I could live with that. Having a part of Lucy was better than nothing. I would have to be careful if I didn't want to lose her, and I really didn't want to lose her.

From the smile on her face when she saw me I knew that I was in with a chance, just as long as I played my cards right. I'd learned a thing or two about Lucy in the previous five months and I knew what made her happy. It would be expensive, and sadly for me her other bloke was clearly streets ahead of me in that department.

She brought the car to a halt just inches from where I was standing and leaned over to open the passenger door.

'Do you need a lift?' she said with a broad smile on her face.

I saw her bag sitting on the back seat so I opened the rear door and put my own battered box suitcase next to her monogrammed leather overnight bag. Lucy was watching me over her shoulder with a smile that curled just one side of her mouth and had a promise of a good time in her eyes. My throat tightened as I realised the enormity of the step that I was about to take.

I should have grabbed my bag and told her that I had to go home to my wife. I should have apologised, begged her forgiveness and taken the backlash from her father and my bosses. Instead I climbed into the front passenger seat and breathed in the smell of Lucy's perfume and the leather of the car's seats.

It might seem odd to say this but part of me was grateful to the other bloke, whoever he was, for lending us his car. It was luxurious beyond my wildest dreams. I wondered if he knew why Lucy wanted it but I thought that was very unlikely. I doubted that he'd be happy sharing his lady with someone like me.

She put the car into gear and we began to move gently and silently away from the curb.

Lucy drove us to the B&B. I would have loved to have had a drive of the car – it would probably be the only chance I ever got – but it just didn't seem right, not seeing as I thought it belonged to another man that she was seeing. I was tempted to question her about the 'friend' that owned the car but in the end I decided not to. Look, I'm not stupid, I knew that I didn't have a lot to offer her, I've never known what she saw in me and I didn't know how long it would be before she got bored of me. Maybe she was already getting bored of me. I decided all I could really do was sit back and enjoyed the ride. I was supposed to be navigating but to be honest there wasn't a lot of that to do. Basically you get on the York road, keep going for about ten miles and there you are, The Paradise View Hotel and Bar.

There was a small car park to the rear and Lucy had her choice of the six or seven spaces on offer.

She turned the engine off and we shared a smile. I was tempted to tell her that I loved her. The words were on the tip of my tongue. But the moment was lost when Lucy opened the driver's door and started to get out. By the time I joined her outside she was looking up at the hotel.

I took the bags from the back seat and we walked around the front to the main entrance. Lucy didn't say anything but she smiled at me when she caught me looking at her so I guessed that what she saw had met with her approval.

There was no-one at the desk but there was a bell which I rang and a minute or two later a woman appeared.

'May I help you?' she asked.

'Yes,' I said, feeling nervous. There was something about the way that she was looking at us, well me really. She had glanced at Lucy, looked her up and down for a second or two, but she was staring at me. 'We have a reservation.'

The woman looked in the book that sat open on the desk. 'Name please.'

'Patterson,' I told her, 'Mr and Mrs Patterson.'

The woman kept her head down as she glanced at Lucy's hand. I thanked God that she'd had the foresight to put a gold band on the third finger of her left hand. She raised her head and looked at me again. I could tell from the look on her face that what appeared to be a wedding ring did nothing to convince her that we were married. However when she gave me the book to sign I could see from the book that we appeared to be the only booking she had for that day, so beggars couldn't be choosers.

'You are in room three,' she said as she handed me a key that was attached to a large wooden key ring with the number of our room chiselled into it. 'It's at the top of the stairs and the first room on the left.' She didn't offer to help us with our bags, not that I would have allowed her to carry them given that she must have been sixty if she was a day, but the offer would have been nice. I'd put the bags down while we waited for our hostess so I picked them up again and started to move towards the stairs. Lucy was a step or two behind me.

'Breakfast is at seven in the dining room,' the woman said when I was on the first step. I looked towards her and noted that she had nodded to a room somewhere behind the glass door on the right. 'If you want anything tonight, there's a pub that does food about half a mile down the road, but mind, out of respect to other guests, we ask that you don't make any noise when you come back and the door is locked at ten o'clock sharp.'

I forced a smile, not that she saw it because she was walking away before she'd finished talking.

The room itself was charming. There was a large wardrobe against one wall and a double bed against the other. There was a floral scent in the air but as there wasn't a flower in sight I put it down to a cleaning product. I wished that I had asked for there to be flowers in the room. I thought Lucy would have appreciated flowers. Maybe next time.

'Here we are then, Mr Patterson' Lucy said through her smile. She had her hand on my chest and she was looking up into my face.

'Here we are Mrs Patter...' she kissed me before I could finish.

Five minutes later we were in bed.

151

I wasn't surprised to see that we were the only ones in the dining room the following morning. I coughed to try and get someone's attention but Lucy took the matter in hand by asking, 'Shall we sit by the window darling?' Our host appeared a few seconds later.

'Good morning,' she said, 'I'm sorry, I didn't hear you.'

She asked us what we wanted for breakfast and we both said full English. It's not something I have very often but I thought that morning qualified as a special occasion.

The woman disappeared back into whatever was behind the door she had come through. Lucy reached across the table and took my hand.

'I loved waking up with you this morning,' she said.

I tried to smile at her. I'd slept badly and when I woke up my first thought had been of Isobel. I despised myself. Or did I? I'm telling you that I did and I was telling myself that too but if I truly did would I have spent the night with Lucy? You have to believe me when I say that I was helpless to stop what was happening. Lucy was a drug and I was addicted to her.

We didn't say a lot but every now and then Lucy would smile at me. It was like she was topping up my dose.

When she brought our breakfasts the woman asked us how we'd slept and I said something like fine or good. Then she turned to Lucy and asked, 'How about you Mrs Patterson?' and I saw something in Lucy's eyes that made me think she was going to come back at her with a smart remark. Lucy wasn't used to being scrutinised like that, not by the likes of B&B landladies, probably not by anyone.

152

Anyway they locked eyes, you know, the way women do when they're having a standoff and after a second or two Lucy gave her best sweet smile and said, 'I slept very well thank you. I find I always do after I've had some exercise.'

I saw the woman's lips twist into a knot as she glared at Lucy, not that Lucy noticed because she was looking out of the window with a smile on her face.

'What?' Lucy asked when we were alone. 'Why are you looking at me like that?'

She was trying to be coy but it's the one thing that she could never pull off, not really.

'Exercise?' I picked up my knife and fork and prepared to attack my food. 'Is that what they call it these days?'

'Well I didn't want to give her a heart attack by saying we'd had rampant sex all night. Poor woman probably hasn't had any since God knows when. I didn't want to make her jealous.' She was laughing as she spoke. 'I'll bet she's going to burn the bedding as it is.'

She'd called it rampant sex and I had to admit it had been rather good, I had been rather good. What can I say, Lucy brought something out in me, something that I couldn't be when I was with Isobel. And I know that makes it sound like I'm blaming Isobel and I'm not, but it's just that sex was different with Lucy. Maybe it was the sex that was the drug.

Lucy looked at the food that had been placed in front of her. She moved everything on the plate around with her fork, like she was looking for something. Turned out she was. 'Bet the old witch has spit in it,' she said.

153

Either she didn't find anything that shouldn't be there or she didn't care because she tucked into her breakfast with gusto. All that rampant sex must have given her an appetite.

After breakfast we packed our things and checked out. I paid for the room and we put the bags in the back of the car.

'We don't have to go home just yet, do we?' she said as she settled down behind the wheel. 'Couldn't we go for a drive first?'

'Won't your friend mind?' I can't tell you how hard it was to make that sentence sound casual.

'Oh no,' she laughed, 'Thomas…ina won't mind at all.'

So I had my answer. His name was Thomas. I could tell from the way that she elongated the name, adding the bit on the end as she had almost tripped herself up. Bentley Boy was called Thomas. *Oh what the hell* I thought, *it's not my petrol allowance we're using up.*

'That would be lovely,' I said.

'Hello darling,' Isobel greeted me at the door like she had been waiting for me. I'd worn the watch that Lucy had bought me while I was away but of course that was buried deep in my bag by then so I had no idea what the time was. Had I even said when I would be back? Was I late?

'Hello,' I said as she pecked my cheek. Instead of pulling away though, she lingered by my face and I could hear the gentle noise of her sniffing the air. I looked at her, 'you alright?'

'What's that smell?' she asked.

154

'What smell?' I honestly didn't know what she was talking about.

'I don't know,' she was sniffing as she spoke, 'it's sort of... floral.'

Shit. 'Oh that's just Wilkin's cologne. He overdid it a bit last night and he smelt of fag ash and beer. He didn't want his wife to know so he's doused himself in half a bottle of cologne to try and cover it up.'

For a second I thought she was eying me suspiciously but then she smiled. 'Well it's very effeminate smelling cologne if he doesn't mind me saying so. More primrose than pine.' She left it at that and turned towards the kitchen. 'Have you eaten?' she asked as she glanced over her shoulder. 'I've got some chops in the fridge.'

I told her that I hadn't eaten and that the thought of her cooking had sustained me through the day. She went to the kitchen and I went upstairs to change and unpack.

LUCY

Thomas is such a flash so and so. Everything has to be the best. But you can afford it of course when your father is one of the richest men in England. Well that's what he says, but he talks rubbish sometimes. His father is very rich though, in fact he makes my father look like a pauper in comparison.

Thomas thinks nothing of paying as much as fifty or sixty pounds for a suit, handmade of course, only the best. So that's why he drives a Bentley, because it's the best. I love it too. You should see the way it turns heads when we drive along in it. When you turn up somewhere in that car you get the best service because people know that you are someone. I knew it would impress Daniel and that was what I was relying on.

Do you know what the funny thing is? It wouldn't matter a jot to Thomas if I wrapped his car round a tree. To him it was just a symbol of his wealth and if I wrecked it he would simply buy another one.

He has an apartment overlooking the river and Robert drove me over there the night before. Thomas had cooked dinner for us; well he'd paid someone to do it for him and when I got there the table was set beautifully and there was a bottle of Chablis in an ice bucket.

The food was delicious but instead of scoffing like I normally do I took by time and nibbled every bite. It wasn't that I wanted to savour the food, it was more a case of putting off what was coming next.

The kissing was bad enough with his wet floppy lips but I knew that he would be expecting more than that if I was going to borrow his Bentley. It wasn't just that he was allowing me to borrow a car he'd paid a fortune for, we had reached that stage in our relationship where he would have expectations.

I'm not going to go into details because I can't even think about it without feeling sick. His hands were everywhere and he was slobbering all over me and all I could think was *dear God please be quick*. Thank goodness it was because it was all I could do to keep my food in my stomach.

It wasn't all bad, though. Afterwards I ran a bubble bath while he sat in a chair smoking cigars and no doubt feeling pleased with himself. As I lay up to my neck in bubbles I looked around his luxurious bathroom and I felt, I don't know how to explain it exactly, I felt at home, like I belonged. I've always been used to the good things in life but Thomas was a step up from what I was used to. I wouldn't mind this life if only I didn't have to put up with the other stuff.

If only he could be more like Daniel in the sex department he would be perfect. Maybe I could get Daniel to give him some lessons. Maybe not.

In the morning he brought me a cup of tea in bed. He had to go to work, for which he apologised, but told me to make myself at home until I had to leave. He left the keys to the car on the bedside table.

I spent the morning lounging around the apartment killing time until I had to go and meet Daniel. I wondered how he had explained a night away from home.

Hopefully Daniel would be on form and the night with him would make up for the one I had endured with Thomas.

I know how this makes me look. I mean I was sleeping with Daniel because my father needed a hold over him though it turned out he was a very good lover and I was sleeping with Thomas who was terrible in bed because he could give me the luxury I craved. The truth is I was only using the things that I had to get what I wanted. I might have had a good education but I'm not a clever person, I don't know things the way some people do. All I have is my name and my looks and that's all I've needed to get my way. You wouldn't be looking at me that way if I were a man.

Anyway, to get back to the point, after I left Thomas' apartment I drove to the 'rendezvous point' – that's what Daniel and I called wherever we were meeting. As I drove around the corner I could see that he was already there.

I could tell that the car had worked because he was so impressed when he saw what I was driving. I had just said that I was borrowing a friend's car, and he probably thought I'd be turning up in an Austin Healey or some other bog standard jalopy but here I was at the wheel of the crème de la crème as the French like to say. I'd wanted it to be a surprise and it was mission accomplished. You should have seen the way he looked at Thomas' car. I don't expect he'd ever seen a Bentley close up before, let alone ridden in one.

I leaned over and opened the door, smiling an invitation to him. I wanted to make it clear that I was going to take him to somewhere he'd never been before and I'm not talking about that geographically.

Daniel gave me directions and I drove to the hotel he had booked. We took the York road for about ten miles or so and we were there. The Paradise View Hotel and Bar. I had to stifle a giggle as we drove into the car park at the back of the hotel because as far as I could see paradise was nowhere in sight. The car park was out of view from the street so I thought the car would be safe enough. It was the only car and I wondered if we would be the only guests.

Maybe Daniel had made a grand gesture and booked the whole place so that we could have a bit of privacy. Perhaps not – I doubted his budget ran to that. More likely it had something to do with that terrible carry on with the petrol rationing. It's a wonder normal people could afford to drive.

Daniel carried the bags towards the main entrance. When he smiled at me he reminded me of a puppy looking to its master to see if they were pleased, so I gave him the smile he was yearning for and he seemed pleased with himself. I've often thought of Daniel as a dog one way or another. I didn't realise that till just now. I like dogs and I liked Daniel. Not the sort of bloke I'd want to spend the rest of my life with but not the worst man I'd had to entertain.

But my heart sank as I looked up at the building. It was hardly the Ritz. The paintwork had definitely seen better days and I thought the sign above the door might have been a bit wonky but my eyesight's not that good so I might be wrong. From the front of the hotel I think I saw the paradise that the name might have been referring to. There were a few trees over the road and a signpost pointing towards a lake. Not much as paradises go. It was hardly the Garden of Eden.

At least it was a step up from The Marsden.

The landlady was a sour faced old crone who looked me up and down. Daniel had booked us in as Mr and Mrs Patterson and lucky for me I'd had the foresight to wear a ring on the third finger of my left hand. Like I told you before, Daniel isn't the first married man I've had a relationship with and I know a thing or two about illicit nights in hotels. I saw her having a crafty glance at my finger when she was supposed to be looking at the register. I don't think she believed that we were married but what could she do? We were paying guests after all and if the car park was anything to go by she'd have taken anyone in.

We had to take our own luggage up to our room which I thought was an absolute disgrace. I don't suppose Daniel would have let her carry our bags anyway but she could at least have shown us to our room. I didn't ask how much Daniel had paid for the room but I hope it wasn't much because it wasn't much of a room. It had a nice enough view of the trees I suppose, but I didn't think much of the lake. I've seen bigger puddles.

The room had a double bed made up with rose printed sheets that matched the curtains and there was a stink of cleaning fluid in the air. I was grateful that it wasn't carbolic. I couldn't have stayed there if they'd used carbolic.

I wouldn't want to embarrass you by going into details but just let me say that we didn't make it anywhere for dinner and there wasn't a lot of sleeping done in the bed.

Consequently I was starving by the morning and could hardly wait for my breakfast. The dining room empty and I don't just mean of guests. There was no sign of the old witch who we had seen the day before. I know we're only talking about a B&B and not a proper hotel but for goodness sake, it really wasn't good enough. I wasn't sure of the normal standards in that sort of place but I really didn't think it was acceptable. Anyway, as there was no-one to tell us where to sit I decided that we would sit at the table in the bay window. It was quite funny actually because *she* appeared then and suggested the same thing.

We ordered our breakfasts and when she brought them she asked how we'd slept. She made a point of calling me Mrs Patterson and emphasised the name just in case I thought she actually believed that we were married. Anyway I couldn't help myself. I can't remember what I said exactly but basically I implied that her bed had seen a lot of use. You should have seen her face. It looked like she'd just sucked on a lemon. She probably burned the bed after we'd left.

I didn't want to go straight home; I wanted to have a little more time together, just the two of us, Mr and Mrs Patterson. Well I didn't really but it was a way of exerting a bit of power and I'm honest enough to tell you that it was all about the power. Has he been that honest?

When I suggested that we go for a drive Daniel asked if my friend would mind and I almost dropped myself in it. I almost said that Thomas wouldn't mind but added 'sina' to the end so you get the name Thomasina. There was a girl called that in my class at school, I never liked her much but I was pleased I remembered her name just in time. I don't think Daniel noticed.

So that's what we did, we drove into the countryside and then we walked for a bit. It was a lovely afternoon and as we walked hand in hand I realised that that's how normal people enjoy themselves. I don't think I'd ever done normal before. It was alright for a little while but I don't think I could live that way. It was a bit dull.

I dropped Daniel off at the park gates where I'd picked him up. I reached over and hugged him and one quick kiss later he was gone and our adventure was over. I looked in the mirror and watched him walk away. I waited until he was round the corner before I started the engine.

I thought about the wife that Daniel would be going home to. I wondered if she would pick up my scent lingering on her husband's clothes. I hoped so because I'd put extra perfume on that morning and made a point of resting against his shirt. I wondered what she would say and how he would explain it.

I often wondered what sort of woman she was, how she was reacting to what was going on. You've got to believe me when I say that I never meant for her to get hurt.

Sorry, I didn't mean to go off track.

After I'd dropped Daniel off, I drove back to Thomas' apartment, parked the car in his spot and put the keys through his letterbox. He's never home before six thirty so I had plenty of time. I walked around the corner to the phone box and called Robert to pick me up.

I often wondered what sort of woman she was, how she
was reacting to what was going on. You've got . . .
me when I say that I never meant for her to get hurt.
Sorry, I didn't mean to go off track.

DANIEL

I've had time to think about what happened and I realise
that things were never the same after that night away. How
could they be when Lucy had such a hold over me? I had to
have her, had to keep her, no matter the cost. And I'm not
just talking financial cost here, though God knows it would
cost me plenty in that respect, but there was the personal
cost too. I knew that Isobel would be devastated if she ever
found out that I had betrayed her, but by that time I was
past caring.

Nothings else mattered. The only thing I cared about
was having Lucy in my life.

I went back to work on the Friday and let Mrs Warren
fuss over me with a steady stream of tea and biscuits. She
claimed that I still looked peaky and wondered if I had
come back to work too early. I thanked her for her concern
and told her that I was fine.

I had nothing scheduled for that morning which gave
me a lot of time to think about our night away. I replayed it
in my head over and over, savouring the moments that we
had shared. I'm not normally what you would call the
romantic type but I felt the need to make some sort of
gesture. I mean I was competing with Bentley Boy for her
affections. I decided to visit the florist during my lunch
break.

Never having done that sort of thing before, once I was in the shop faced with this array of God knows what they were called, I chose this and that and then something else as well. I wanted to impress her. And, when the florist had put them all together and tied them up with a ribbon they looked the part.

The lady in the shop said that she could organise delivery which I already knew because I'd seen the sign in the window and I'd come prepared with the address which I had taken from her father's file. She gave me a card to write on.

I thought *Thank you for the best night of my life* might cause a bit of a stir if her parents saw it so I took a leaf out of her book and just wrote *Thank you*. Without realising it, I started to sign my name. Just as I finished the curve in the 'D' I stopped. What was I doing? I could have kicked myself. By that point it was too late to do anything about it because the florist was looking at me with a puzzled look on her face. I could hardly ask her for another card could I because she would have thought that was very strange. Anyway, she'd have probably charged me an extra two bob. So I just put an 'x' underneath it and made out that everything was fine. She said that they would be delivered that afternoon.

I left the shop and walked back to work thinking of how Lucy would react when she saw what I had bought her. In my head I saw her smiling as she realised they were for her. Then as she read the card she'd get this look in her eye, a look of tenderness or maybe even love.

Did she love me? Did I want her to love me?

I knew that I wanted her to want me as much as I wanted her but was that love or was it just desire? I know I've said that I thought I loved her, so maybe they are the same thing. And I did desire her; more than I ever knew was possible. That night away had been like a dream, a dream that I didn't want to wake up from.

When Isobel had smelled Lucy's perfume on me I'd said the first thing that had come into my head and she had believed it. How could she possibly have thought that it was aftershave that she could smell? Maybe she had known it was perfume but she trusted me enough to put any doubts she might have had out of her mind. Poor trusting Isobel. How could she not see what was going on in front of her? I'm not a good liar... or at least I hadn't been before I met Lucy. I was getting better, but even so, Isobel had been my wife for fifteen years, shouldn't she have been able to read me?

It was a week before I saw Lucy again. The following Thursday evening when I was supposedly at my Gentleman's Club I was really at that place on Silver Street, the one with the French name, eating dinner with Lucy. The French name added about two quid each to the bill, but it was worth it. Lucy had mentioned it in passing that night we were away so I knew that she'd be pleased that I'd made a reservation there. I'd had no need to tell her to dress up because she always did, in fact she was a little over dressed for some of the places I'd taken her in the past but that night she fit right in.

'The flowers were beautiful Daniel,' she purred in a way that sent a shiver down my spine.

'I'm glad you liked them.' I tried to sound casual but I don't think I carried it off.

Over the next couple of months, I sent her flowers four or five times and I signed the cards the same way each time. I thought of it as my calling card. I liked buying her things. She had mentioned that it was her birthday in June and I wanted to get her something special. I bought her a gold necklace with a tear drop shaped sapphire hanging from it. I gave it to her over crème brûlée at Poplar Lodge. I'd been worried about going there but she was adamant that was where she wanted to go. She had said that it was a tradition and I was so happy that she had decided to spend her birthday with me rather than this Thomas bloke that I agreed before she could change her mind. Not that she'd ever come clean about the other fella, but she didn't have to. Like I've already admitted, I would rather have had a piece of her than none of her at all.

How could I be so pathetic?

It was costing me more and more to keep her happy, and I reached the point where I was finding it hard to make ends meet. I earned a decent wage as bank manager, a good wage by most standards, but it wasn't enough. By the end of the month there just wasn't enough money left.

'I love this,' she said as we stood together sheltering from the rain under a tree in the grounds of Poplar Lodge. 'You shouldn't have, though,' she was holding the box I had given her, fingering the necklace as she looked into my eyes, 'it must have been very expensive.'

'Don't worry about it,' I told her and why should she? I was worrying enough for the pair of us.

She had called Robert from the restaurant and I estimated it would take him about fifteen minutes to get there. You can see the Town Hall clock from where we were standing so I was able to gauge how long we had left together. When, after fourteen minutes I saw headlights turning into the drive I knew our time was up so I kissed her, wished her happy birthday one last time, and stepped back into the shadows.

Robert stopped the car just inches from her. He got out and ran around to the passenger side so that he could open the door for her. I heard her thank him as she climbed into the back seat. I watched them drive away and didn't move from my spot until the rear lights were all the way down the drive and out of the gates.

I'd been hiding beside one of the out buildings and it was only as I moved away from it that I realised the guttering must have broken. Rain had leaked from it onto my shoulders and my overcoat felt heavy as I started the walk home.

LUCY

The doorbell rang about three o'clock on the afternoon after we'd got home from our night away. I heard it but I didn't go to answer it. That's what we pay housekeepers for. I was sitting in the lounge with my mother and we could hear Janet, the housekeeper, talking to someone. I think my mother even shouted out to ask who it was but she wasn't particularly interested and didn't even look up from the magazine she was reading. Have you noticed how many times I've told you that my mother was reading a magazine? She spends half her life doing it. It's no wonder my father has strayed.

Anyway, we heard the door close and a few seconds later Janet walked into the room carrying a bunch of flowers. Well it was several bunches by the look of it put together to look like one but they weren't fooling anyone.

Now my mother was interested. 'Are they for me?' she asked, suddenly getting all perky.

'No Mrs Braithwaite, they're for Miss Lucy.' Poor Janet didn't know where to look.

'Really?' my mother said and I wondered who she thought might be sending her flowers.

'Yes,' Janet brought the flowers to me.

I'd been sitting in the corner of the sofa with my feet tucked underneath me so she laid the flowers on my lap and said that she'd bring a vase before disappearing as quickly as she could.

I knew who they were from, of course. Thomas would have sent a bouquet of roses and lilies so I knew they weren't from him. These freesias, carnations and whatever you call those red things with heads like tennis balls had Daniel written all over them. Pretty enough in their own way I suppose.

There was a card with the words, *thank you* written on it and then the initial *D* with a kiss underneath.

'What's it say?' my mother asked, 'who are they from?'

'Just a friend,' I said as I handed them to Janet who had reappeared carrying a vase half full of water. I asked her to put them in my bedroom.

My mother had mentioned the flowers while we were eating supper. She was desperate to know who they were from.

'Got an admirer have we?' my father teased.

'No,' I said, 'they were just from a friend.' I gave my father a knowing look and for the benefit of my mother I said, 'They were from Josie. Just a little thank you for helping her out the other night. For being there for her when she needed me.'

You see on Wednesday I'd told my mother that Josie was having boyfriend trouble and that I was spending the night at her house to give her a shoulder to cry on. She doesn't really know Josie so she didn't know that I wasn't telling her the truth. My father had known where I was, or rather who I was with, but I knew my secret was safe with

170

him. He helped me out by telling us about his day and the flowers were forgotten.

Later, after my mother had gone to bed, my father and I sat together in the lounge having a night cap.

'Where were you on Wednesday?' he asked.

I took a mouthful of gin and let it slip down my throat before I told him, 'A B&B on the York road.'

'Nice?' he asked.

I put my glass on the coffee table and leaned towards him. I kept my voice down because for all my mother had said she was going to bed I wouldn't put it past her to be sitting on the stairs ear wigging on our conversations. 'It was grim, Daddy,' I told him.

'Did he hurt you?' he was keeping his voice low too. I guess he didn't trust my mother any more than I did.

'Oh God no,' I laughed at the thought of it. 'Daniel would never hurt me. I'm afraid he might love me.'

'Well done, darling.' He held up his whiskey glass in a salute. After he'd taken a drink he put his glass on the table near mine. 'You've done very well Lucy. Just a little while longer and we'll be able to send Daniel back to his wife.'

That night as I lay in bed, I looked at the flowers and told myself that they were pretty even if they weren't roses and lilies. I love roses and lilies as a combination.

The following Thursday I met Daniel as usual outside the library and he surprised me by telling me that he had reservations at Le Petit Monde on Silver Street. Have you ever been there? You should go, the food is divine!

171

I'd mentioned it while we were away the week before but I hadn't realised he'd taken any notice of me. I certainly hadn't expected him to take me there because I had no idea that he would be able to afford it. I don't know how much bank managers earned, but I didn't think it gave them the scope to eat at fancy French restaurants. I wondered if he had to dip into some savings to pay for it. In fact part of me hoped that he was because that would strengthen my hand which in turn would strengthen my father's.

I wondered again if Daniel loved me. I thought he must do to spend that sort of money on me, money that he probably didn't have. I was willing to bet that he'd never taken the wife he'd still not told me about there. But you see the thing is that I didn't want him to love me, well maybe I did because everybody wants to be loved. I just hoped that he didn't think that I loved him back.

I know that makes me sound like a cow, which I probably am, but I love money. I love expensive things, nice meals, and I could only love a man who could give those things to me. Daniel was interesting and he was good in bed but he was never going to be my life partner. And, let's be honest, I was only going out with him because my father had told me to. The minute he told me that he was finished with Daniel I'd be finished with him too.

He went a bit soppy eyed when I thanked him for the flowers that he sent. I suppose he thought that I meant it. I'm not saying they weren't nice but they just weren't my sort of flowers. They were more like something you'd stick on your grandma's grave.

Sometime in May, I sort of dropped into conversation that it was my birthday the following month. It was a total lie of course because my birthday's in November but I wanted to test Daniel. We'd started off having quick bunk ups in that flea pit of a hotel and progressed to slightly better, though still not really up to my standards, hotels for a few hours of illicit passion. Our first meal together had been that ham broth in the café on the corner and now we had eaten the glorious food that places like Le Petit Monde had to offer. We'd even had a night away. We had come a long way in a few short months.

My father had implied more than once that my relationship with Daniel would be coming to an end shortly so I had to get what I could while I could.

I remembered the bracelet that Daniel had bought me, the one that had never seen the light of day since I threw it into the back of my knicker drawer and I wanted to see what he would buy me now.

I thought it was odd when he asked me if he would see me on my birthday. I'd chosen the twentieth specifically because it was a Thursday. I told him that there was no-one else that I would rather spend my birthday with and I thought he was going to burst with happiness.

'The thing is, Daniel,' I said slowly, making it sound like I was reluctant to say what I was going to say. 'I have this… tradition on my birthday.' I paused for effect before adding, 'I normally go to Poplar Lodge.' Another total lie.

On my last birthday I'd been up to London with a couple of friends to see a show.

Daniel accepted the lie as gospel truth and said that if that was the tradition then he would book a table.

If he was trying to impress me it worked because I was fully aware of how much he was going to have to spend on me. I just hoped that he wouldn't think that the meal was my present. I would find that very disappointing.

We had a table for two in the corner by the piano and it was lovely, no honestly it was. We ordered our food and when the waiter asked if we would like wine Daniel asked him to recommend something to 'complement the food.' Well, Jonathan picked what is probably the second most expensive bottle of wine that they have, a chardonnay with a good vintage. Daniel went with the recommendation and to be honest it did complement our food beautifully but I saw Daniel's eyes glaze over a little bit at the end of the evening when he got the bill.

Naturally I had crème brûlée for dessert and so did Daniel. That was when he slid the box across the table to me.

'Happy birthday Lucy,' he said.

He had bought me a gold chain with a sapphire drop hanging from it. The sapphire was very small but at least it looked real.

I'd called Robert from the restaurant and he said he was on his way. That's the lovely thing about Robert; whenever I call he comes running.

It was raining when we left the restaurant and we sheltered under one of the trees that line the drive to Poplar Lodge as we waited for Robert to arrive. I took the necklace out of my handbag and told him that I loved it. I told him that it must have been expensive and that he shouldn't have. He told me not to worry about it, which was good because I wasn't.

When headlights appeared at the end of the driveway Daniel kissed me quickly and slipped into the shadows of one of the out-buildings.

It was raining when we left the restaurant and we sheltered under one of the trees that line the driveway lodge as we waited for Robert to arrive. I took the necklace out of my handbag and told him that I loved it.

DANIEL

As I walked home I started to think about what my life had become. Once upon a time I was a simple uncomplicated genial bank manager. Now I had become someone else entirely. The old me wouldn't have got into bed, metaphorically speaking, with a man like Arthur Braithwaite, and he certainly wouldn't have actually got into bed with the man's daughter.

But I had, I had become a person that I barely recognised anymore.

I realised just how much I'd changed the following day.

Knowing what I was doing to her, I could no longer stand the sight of Isobel's face across the breakfast table, so I made an excuse and left for work early. She was used to it so I don't suppose she even gave it a second thought.

About ten o'clock the phone rang and Mrs Warren asked if she could put Mr Braithwaite through. I said she could but it took me a second or two to get the words out.

'Good morning, Mr Braithwaite,' I said as soon as the connection was made, 'this is a surprise.'

'Well Danny Boy,' he said, 'the thing is, I think I need to have a little chat with you.'

What could he want? Why did we need a chat? The questions ran through my head one after the other. I could feel the perspiration start to form on my forehead and I put my hand over my mouth and stared at a spot on the carpet. I made a noise that wasn't a word. 'So how about you come over to my office, Danny?' he sounded jovial enough but that did nothing to calm the feeling in my stomach.

'Can you tell me what this is about please?' It was a standard question for this sort of request but I was almost scared to hear the answer.

'I'd rather not say on the phone if you don't mind Danny,' he said. 'You know what they say about walls having ears. How's two o'clock for you?'

'Today?' The urgency worried me.

He said that he wanted to 'deal with the matter' as soon as possible so yes today, if that was alright.

Two o'clock it was then.

I walked to the door and Mrs Warren stopped typing and looked at me. A look of concern spread over her face and she pushed her chair back. 'Mr Laither,' she said. 'Whatever is the matter?'

'Nothing,' I said trying to pull myself together, 'I just came over a little queasy, that's all.'

'Would you like me to get you a cup of tea to settle your stomach?'

'Thank you that would be lovely. Oh and by the way, I just wanted to tell you that I'll need you to cancel my afternoon appointments, I need to go out.'

I don't think she realised that she glanced at the telephone. 'Very well sir,' she said as she disappeared towards the kitchen.

I didn't like it when she called me sir.

I went back to my desk and had recovered a little by the time she arrived with the tea. As she put it down she looked at my diary that was sitting open on the desk and read the name '*Arthur Braithwaite*' alongside two o'clock. She looked at me and although she didn't actually shake her head she might as well have.

I arrived at his office a little before two and the lovely Miss Monroe asked me to take a seat. 'He'll not be a minute,' she said. 'Can I get you anything while you wait?'

I said she couldn't and she went back to doing whatever it was that she'd been doing before I walked in.

I was looking at the floor when the door to Braithwaite's office opened. I turned my head expecting to see the man himself but instead was greeted by the sight of Robert filling the doorway. He'd looked big on the occasions that I'd seen him from a distance but close up he was enormous. He held his head up so that his nose was in the air. When he looked in my direction he was literally looking down his nose at me.

'Thank you very much Robert,' I heard Arthur say, 'Really appreciate it.' I caught a glimpse of his boss behind him.

As Robert walked away Arthur took his place. He didn't fill the doorway quite as much as Robert had but it wasn't far off.

'Danny,' he said, 'good to see you. Sorry to keep you waiting, won't you come in?' He seemed everything the admired businessman should be, so why did I have a horrible feeling in my stomach?

I walked into his office though for the life of me I don't know how my legs carried me.

He'd asked Miss Monroe to bring us some tea and then said that we would wait until it arrived before we got started. I didn't understand why he would do that because by their very nature private secretaries are privy to all sorts of confidential information and often walk in on private conversations. I wondered if he was just enjoying watching me sweat.

Miss Monroe seemed to be taking a long time to make the tea and I wondered if she had been instructed to do that. I realised that I was probably just being paranoid but that didn't change anything.

As we waited in silence all I could think was that Robert had seen me the night before and reported that I had been lurking in the bushes watching Lucy. I suspected that Arthur took that sort of thing badly so maybe he wanted to mark my cards. I just hoped he didn't mark my face too much.

Eventually the tea arrived and when the door was finally closed with Miss Monroe on the other side of it Arthur leaned forward with his elbows set wide on the desk and his hands joined together.

'So... Danny,' he said. 'You're probably wondering what's so important that I asked you to come here at such short notice.' He was staring at me across the desk, daring me to look away first. He pushed himself back into his chair, 'The thing is Danny, I need some more money.'

What? This was about money? I let out the breath that I'd been holding and hoped it didn't sound as loud as it felt. I had to cough to get my voice working. 'I don't understand.'

He picked up the tea cup and I noticed that he held the whole thing in his hand rather than try to get his fingers through the hole of the handle. He drained the cup in one.

'The factory I'm building,' he wiped the back of his hand across his lips, 'the one I got the loan for, well it's going to cost more than I originally thought. I'm going to need to extend my line of credit.'

This was almost as bad as being told that he knew about me and Lucy. I'd already gone out on a limb with the bank to get him the original loan and here he was asking for more. I know I hadn't initiated these dealings but it had occurred to me that it was my name on Arthur's original loan agreement, and if William Morris chose to he could say that he knew nothing about it. He could say that he didn't even know Arthur Braithwaite let alone that he had asked me to help him out. I was the one taking all the risks and now he was asking me to take another. Except he wasn't really asking was he?

I swallowed hard, 'How much more?'

'Ten thousand pounds.' Somehow he managed to make it sound like a small amount of money.

'On top of the fifteen thousand that you have already borrowed?' It wasn't a small amount of money and I wanted to clarify that I'd understood him correctly.

'Yes,' he paused. 'Not going to be a problem, is it?'

Over the course of the next ten minutes he explained that he would want the loan as an extension of the one he had taken out in November, same terms, same rate of interest.

'Come on now Danny,' he said as I hesitated, 'I thought you wanted the chair in the shiny new branch on the high street. Bill Morris did tell you that was his plan for you didn't he? Think of all the money this will make for the shareholders, and not only that, think of all the jobs that you'll be helping to create, all the families that will want to come and deposit their wages in your bank.' He let the statement hang there for a second or two before he said, 'Oh, and by the way, Lucy says hello.' His eyes said more than his words ever could.

If the terror I was feeling showed in my eyes he didn't say anything. I wasn't there to get a beating for deflowering his daughter but I could tell that he knew. And what's more he was willing to use that information to get what he wanted. He'd mentioned the shareholders, which to me meant that he was willing to go to them if I didn't give him what he wanted. He'd also mentioned Lucy, and while I had no worry that he would hurt her if I didn't give him what he wanted, he was using her as a threat.

'I'm very close to Lucy, you know,' he said. 'When one of us is happy so is the other one. She seems really happy

at the moment, happier than I've seen her in a long time.'
He smiled at me for a few seconds. 'It does my old heart
the world of good to see her so happy. I can't bear to see
her sad.'

By the time I left his office I had agreed to have some
paper work drawn up that I would get back to him within a
few days. As I walked the short distance back to the bank I
didn't know which felt worse, my arm up my back or the
noose around my neck.

LUCY

Robert wasn't much of a talker, not around me anyway, so I was surprised when he asked me about my evening. 'Did you have a nice time Miss Braithwaite?'

I was looking out of the window as he spoke, looking at the spot where Daniel was standing in the shadows. I could pick him out because I knew he was there but I doubted anyone else would be able to see him. 'Yes, very nice thank you Robert,' my breath clouded the window when I answered him. I wasn't looking at him as I spoke but when I turned my eyes to the front I saw that Robert was looking at me through the mirror. The headlights of a passing car lit up his face and I could see that he was staring at me. I thought that there was something a bit sinister about the way he'd asked his question, and for the first time I saw why my father used Robert when he thought he needed protection. Sorry, I realise that makes it sound like my father is some sort of gangster who needs a bodyguard, but what I mean is that I could see why you would want Robert on your side in a tight corner. He's a sweetheart, really – he just looks mean.

He didn't say anything else to me during the journey home.

When he stopped the car outside the house he was around the car and opening the door before I'd managed to get myself together. For such a big man Robert is remarkably quick on his feet. I thanked him and went towards the front door. He waited until I was inside the house before he got back in the car and drove away.

My father was in the living room sitting on one end of the sofa. There was a glass of whiskey resting on the arm. He had been reading some papers but he put them down and patted the seat beside him.

'Fancy a night cap?' he asked. I'm never known to turn one down so he didn't wait for my answer and was on his way to the drinks cabinet before he'd finished asking the question. As he was pouring my drink he also asked me if I had had a good evening.

'It was Poplar Lodge,' I laughed, 'so what do you think?'

'I think it must have cost him a pretty penny.' He held up his glass and I chinked mine against his.

'He bought me a birthday present,' I said as I pulled the box out of my handbag and handed it to him.

'Nice,' he nodded his head as he took the necklace out of the box. He has really big fingers so it was a bit lost in his hands. He held the sapphire up to his eyes. 'Small but real,' he smiled, 'he really has a thing for you.' He dropped it back in the box and gave it back to me. 'We have him just where we want him.'

184

DANIEL

It must have been after three before I got back to the bank because I noticed that everyone was starting to wind the day down ready for closing the doors at three thirty. I hadn't gone straight back to work; I'd wandered around the streets for a bit trying to get my head straight.

He was asking too much of me. How on earth was I supposed to extend his credit by ten thousand pounds? Five hundred I could have got away with, maybe even a thousand, but ten thousand...? No, it couldn't be done.

William Morris had asked me to do him one favour and I had done that. There had been no mention of anything after that initial transaction and I wondered if he was aware of what his mate Arthur was asking for. Should I ring and ask him for advice? I'd feel happier if he sanctioned this second loan. I mean, with interest rates as low as they were anyway I thought the board would take a very dim view of me agreeing to make them even lower. Somehow that chair in the shiny new High Street branch seemed further away than ever.

Things would have been easier if I didn't love Lucy. There, I've said it, and why not, it's true. I loved Lucy.

'Excuse me Mr Laither but I did knock.'

I was surprised by the sound and when I looked up I saw that Mrs Warren was standing about a foot away from my desk. I hadn't heard her knock and I certainly hadn't seen her walk in.

'Are you alright Daniel?' she asked kindly. It was so unlike her to use my Christian name. I know I've told you that I had a more familiar relationship with her than the others, but even so she rarely called me anything other than Mr Laither. She only called me 'Sir' if she was angry with me.

'Yes,' I said, 'I'm fine Mrs Warren, why shouldn't I be?' I said sharply.

'It's just that you don't seem yourself... sir.' She emphasised the last word and I realised that I must have hurt her when I'd thrown her kindness back in her face. I was sorry for that because Ida Warren is one of the nicest people I know. She has never been anything but kind to me and I know that she watched my back every day. Young Bridge was ambitious and wanted my job and she always made sure that I was one step ahead of him.

'I'm sorry,' I said, and I meant it.

'That's alright,' she sat down and rested her hands in her lap. 'Is there anything I can do for you?'

'No,' I tried to force a smile onto my face, 'honestly I'm fine.' I don't think she believed me but she didn't press the point. However she remained sitting and when I looked at her I saw that she was nibbling her bottom lip. 'Is there something wrong?' I asked.

'There was a phone call this afternoon from Head Office,' she said slowly. It wasn't unusual for phone calls from the inner sanctum but there was something about the way Mrs Warren announced it that made it sound out of the ordinary. I felt my throat tighten.

'Was there a message?' I croaked.

'It's Mr Morris,' she said and my throat tightened even further. I don't know what I thought she was going to say but I was totally unprepared for the words, 'he's dead.'

Dead? How could he be dead? She said that she didn't know all of the details, just that it had been sudden.

So that was it, I was alone. I know that he hadn't been much support up to that point and I had my doubts that he would have backed me up but at least there had been a chance that he would. That chance had gone.

Apparently I didn't speak much that evening, Isobel commented on it as we were going up the stairs to bed. I didn't sleep much either.

There was no other way around it so I called Mrs Warren into my office the following morning. I'd written down all of the figures and I gave them to her.

'I want you to draw up the paperwork as soon as possible please and bring it directly to me for approval. It's not to go through Bridge, in fact, this is between us.'

She looked at me sceptically, 'Are you sure these figures are correct?'

I had to run my tongue over the inside of my mouth to moisten it. 'Yes.'

She stood up slowly, 'I'll have them ready by lunch time,' she said.

She paused as she opened the door and I thought that she was going to say something else but she didn't, she just turned and looked at me and I thought that I could see something in her eyes. I think it was disappointment.

I was becoming someone else and Mrs Warren could see that.

But the thing about Ida is that she's like the dog we had when I was a kid. I mean that in a good way. He would have laid down his life for me and Ida Warren was the same. She was loyal.

She handed me the paperwork at about half eleven and then said that she needed to go home. She said that she didn't feel very well. I told her that I hoped she would be better soon and sent her on her way. I told her to get a taxi and I would pay for it but she said she would be fine on the bus.

I knew what I was doing was wrong but I didn't know how not to do it. I've just admitted to you that I loved Lucy and I was willing to do anything to keep her, and to keep her I needed to keep her happy. She would only stay interested in me if I could keep her happy. Thomas, I was sure that was his name even though she had never actually told me, could buy her things and that would make her happy. The only thing I had that her friend with the Bentley didn't was my ability to offer her father credit. Lucy loved her father very deeply so keeping him happy would keep her happy too.

It was just the interest rate thing. He was using his power over me to extort a ridiculously low rate and how could I not go along with it? Even if you take Lucy out of the equation I still couldn't refuse him because all he would have to do would be to tell my superiors about the terms of the first loan. Can you imagine what their response would have been if I said that a dead man had told me to do the deal with him?

I'd never respected him as a man but now I despised him.

I took the contract over to Braithwaite's office that afternoon.

'Terrible news about Bill,' he said as I rifled through my briefcase for the paperwork. 'I didn't even know he was ill.' I thought I saw the hint of a smile on his face.

'It was very sudden,' I said as I handed him the contract, 'It's come as a shock to us all.'

He looked at the papers briefly.

'I knew you'd see things my way Danny,' he said as he signed his name on the dotted line. As he screwed the top back on his fountain pen he added, 'You'll not regret this,' and I thought that it was too bloody late for that.

Between my desire to keep Lucy in my life and my need to keep my dealings with her father a secret from my bosses I was in way over my head. Who am I kidding? I always had been.

So that was June-July time and by the August I'd just about run out of money and I'd resorted to taking out a loan. I was up against a bloke who had a Bentley for God's sake and that sort of thing costs more than I earned.

189

Have you any idea how much a meal costs in Poplar Lodge, or that French place? No I don't suppose you do because people like us aren't meant for places like that, but Lucy was. That was the world she was used to and if I was going to keep her, one way or another that was the world that I had to give her.

There was this one time that she arrived one Thursday evening wearing a necklace that I had never seen before. Something told me that it had been a present from my rival. Do you know what I did? I went out the following day and bought her a bracelet that would match it. What was wrong with me? I can't even bring myself to tell you how much that bracelet cost.

I realised that I'd reached rock bottom financially when Isobel asked for a cheque one morning. She said that she needed to buy an anniversary present for Sylvia and Stephen. She'd seen something somewhere that she said would be perfect for them but said she would rather pay by cheque than cash. Just as well really because I had no cash to give her, not until pay day anyway.

She was prattling on about what she was going to buy and I wanted to tell her to shut up. Just thinking about money and the mess I was in caused me enough of a headache without actually talking about it. I remember making a comment about the present being a bit expensive and she laughed and told me not to be a skinflint. She reminded me that they were our oldest friends. She said they were 'almost family.' She'd thought I was joking you see. That just made everything even worse, if such a thing is possible. Anyway I signed the cheque and gave it to her to fill out at the store but I knew that I had to get some money in my account before the cheque cleared. Can you imagine what would have happened if my cheque had bounced?

I couldn't get a loan from the bank, because I'm sure you can see the problem with that, me being a bank manager and all. There was no way that I could give myself the loan without Ida or, God forbid, Bridge finding out what I had done and that would be the end of my career. I couldn't even go to a colleague because they would ask what I wanted the loan for and I could hardly say that I wanted it to finance an affair I was having.

There was only one other option.

I made a call in the morning and during my lunch break I went to see a man called Jack McGuire. We were in the same line of work in many ways except his branch of business wasn't quite so legitimate if you get my meaning. We'd known each other a long time and his brother Billy had been in the same class as me and Stephen.

'Never expected to see you in here, Danny,' he said. He was wearing the same sort of flash suit that Arthur Braithwaite favoured so clearly business was good.

'Never expected to be here, Jack,' I told him.

'So, what can I do for you?' He waved towards a chair.

'What do you think?' I brushed what looked like cat hairs off the chair before I sat down.

I walked away from his 'office' twenty minutes later with a wad of cash in my pocket along with a piece of paper that said I would make a repayment to him every week until I had paid back three times what I had borrowed.

That wasn't my intention of course. My plan was that I'd clear the debt in a few weeks, two months, maximum. I told myself that this was just a temporary cash flow problem.

There'd been our night away, the meals in that French place and her birthday on top of that. There'd just been a lot of expenses in a very short period of time, that was all. The loan from Jack was only ever intended to be a stop gap.

I was able to deposit the cash in my account that day meaning that there would be plenty to cover the cheque that Isobel would be writing for whatever the hell it was she was buying.

You know what it's like though, and the more you do the more is expected of you. I'd taken Lucy to a couple of nice restaurants and now she expected it all the time. It was costing me a bloody fortune.

Needless to say, when the payments came due I didn't have the money. The first time it happened I was given a bit of leeway, Jack just said to make sure that I could pay the next week. When the next week came he said that things were getting more serious and that there would be consequences if it happened again. Come the next week I was still unable to pay Jack the money I owed him so I had a fair idea of what would be coming next. My previous relationship with Jack would only buy me so much time and I was rapidly running out of it.

Have you any idea how embarrassing that is? I'm a *bank manager*.

I ran out of time one Wednesday. I was walking away from the bank when two men barred my path. They had 'heavies' written all over them. Both of them were built like brick outhouses in suits and each had a nose that had been broken more than once. I knew who they were, or rather, who had sent them.

'Danny Laither?' one of them asked.

I don't know what possessed me but I corrected him, telling him that my name was Daniel.

'Danny Laither,' he said again. He emphasised the name this time as he moved to my side and put an arm around my shoulder. He did this so that he could manoeuvre me more easily. I'm going to say that we walked around the back of the bank but I didn't have any choice in where we were going. He had practically lifted me off my feet. The other man was walking a couple of steps behind us, there to grab me if I was stupid enough to make a run for it. The chance would have been a fine thing. I was trapped.

Once we were out of sight the one who had had his arm around my shoulder turned me around to face him and with his face just a couple of inches away from mine he said, 'You got what we want, Danny?' There was a hint of whiskey on his breath but I don't think that was what made me feel sick. 'I asked you a question, Danny.' He wasn't shouting, but he didn't need to. His voice was full of spit and menace. He raised an eyebrow like he was expecting an answer but I couldn't speak. What would be the point? I wasn't going to be able to reason with him.

I was on the floor after the second punch which made it easier for them to land their kicks in my stomach. I don't know how long the beating actually took but it felt like a lifetime, and when it was over I could hardly breathe. One of my eyes was closed and I could taste blood in my mouth.

'That was just a warning,' I heard one of them say, 'don't make us come back again because we won't be so gentle next time.' I heard the sound of their feet walking away. After a few steps they stopped and I was terrified that they were coming back for more. I was relieved that they didn't but they had a parting message for me. I heard the words, 'Jack's still going to want his money,' and then laughter. I tried to lift my head off the concrete but it hurt too much.

A man walking his dog found me like that some time later. His Jack Russell started licking my face as I heard someone say. 'Bloody hell pal, are you alright? Stay there while I call the police.'

'No,' I started to say, 'I'll be alright.' The last thing I wanted was him calling the police so I opened my eyes and forced myself off the floor. I didn't get far at first because every part of me ached, but five minutes later I was standing.

'You sure you don't want me to call the police?' he said. This stranger seemed genuinely concerned for me and I was touched by it. Help thy neighbour and all that.

'No,' I insisted, 'I'll be fine,' though I wasn't sure I would be. 'What would be the point? I can't tell them anything.'

'What? You have no idea who did it to you?'

'No,' I said as I pulled my handkerchief out of my pocket and dabbed my swollen lip, 'they just came out of nowhere.'

'Were you taking a short cut?' he asked sceptically and even through my half closed eye I could see the doubt on his face. The short cut he was referring to was a muddy lane leading to an even muddier field that brought you to the back of the dance hall and there was no way I would have taken that route dressed as I was in a suit and brogues.

'No,' I said trying to force my shoulders back. I remember hearing the bones in my back creak as I did it. 'I was walking along the street, on my way home after work when the next thing I knew I was being forced around that corner and once we were in this yard they set about me.'

'So you didn't you get a look at them?' Was it really so hard to believe?

I wondered if my saviour was actually an off duty police officer. That'd be just my luck wouldn't it?

'No,' I started to walk away but stumbled on the first step and had to lean against the wall to get my balance back. The man went to grab me but I held up my hand to show him that I was fine. I didn't need anyone making a fuss. 'It all happened too quickly,' I said as I composed myself again, 'and then, once I was on the floor, all I could see were their boots.'

'Did they steal anything?' The dog was starting to pull on its lead and I wished he would take notice of it and disappear.

It occurred to me that they might have taken my wallet to at least get back some of the money that I owed Jack, but I tapped my pocket and found that it was still there. 'No,' I said, 'everything's where it should be.'

'What about the hospital?' he asked. His dog was starting to get really bored by that point and was pulling even harder on his lead.

'I'll go and see my doctor,' I told him. 'I'll go home and get cleaned up and then I'll call my doctor.'

'Do you need a hand getting home?' He asked the question but I don't think it was a genuine offer.

'No, I'll be fine,' I assured him. 'Thank you very much for all your trouble.'

The man and his dog went one way and I staggered the other.

'Oh my God,' Isobel's screech almost perforated my eardrums. 'What on earth has happened to you?' She came rushing forward and helped me into the dining room and sat me on a chair which came as a blessed relief because I don't think I could have stood much longer.

'It's nothing,' I tried to make a joke of it, 'it looks worse than it is.'

She asked me what had happened and I told her the same story that I had told the man with the dog. I said I'd been walking along the street on my way home from work when I was suddenly forced down an alley and beaten up by unidentified assailants.

'Did you call the police?' Poor Isobel, she looked like she was going to be sick.

'No,' I told her, 'what was the point? I couldn't have identified the least thing about them and they didn't steal anything.'

'Why?' I saw a tear roll down her cheek. 'Why would someone do this to you, Daniel?'

'I don't know,' I said. 'Wrong place at the wrong time I suppose.'

Isobel bathed my cuts and generally cleaned me up, and then settled me down in the chair by the fire and brought me my tea on a tray. We always sat at the dining table for meals but she made an exception that night. Thank God it was Shepherd's Pie which I could shovel into my mouth and swallow without having to move too many muscles. I don't think I could have managed anything that I had to chew. All the while I was eating she sat in the chair on the opposite side of the fire and nibbled at her own food. She didn't eat much, just pushed it around with her fork really.

After I'd eaten all that I wanted she took my plate away and returned about ten minutes later with two cups of tea. I could feel her watching me, just looking, searching for an explanation. When she couldn't get the answer she wanted just by looking at me she asked me.

'Why?'

I looked at her but found that I couldn't hold her eyes, so I lowered my own and looked at my tea instead. I saw a stray tea leaf floating on the top of it. It was all alone just moving from side to side with no control over where it went or what happened to it. I knew just how it felt. *You are a tealeaf Daniel* I thought.

'Why Daniel,' Isobel asked the question again. 'Why would someone beat you up?'

'I don't know,' I whispered.

'I could understand if it was a robbery, it wouldn't make it right but I could understand it.' I didn't answer her and I could still feel her watching me. I don't think I have ever felt more uncomfortable in my life. I heard her lift her cup from its saucer and a few seconds later set it down again. 'But what I really don't understand is why you won't tell the police.' Without realising that I had lifted my head I was looking into her eyes. 'Why won't you go to the police, Daniel?'

'It's like I said before, what would be the point? I didn't see who did it and nothing was taken.' The words didn't sound like they were coming out right through my swollen lips but Isobel appeared to understand me. 'Look love,' I tried to smile but I don't think I pulled it off. 'When it happened all I wanted was for it to end and after it had, I just wanted to come home,' I left a pause there before adding, 'to you. I didn't want to talk to police about it when I knew full well that there was nothing they could do about catching whoever had done it. All I wanted was to come home to you.' I could see her face softening and the next thing I knew, her cup and saucer were on the floor and so was she. She sat on the floor, resting her hand on my thigh.

'Oh Daniel,' she said, 'I can't bear that someone did this to you. I love you so much.' She put her head in my lap and I stroked her hair.

I felt a complete bastard.

I slept fitfully and woke up feeling just as bad as I had the night before. Isobel said that I wasn't fit to go to work and she was right. After breakfast, which she served to me in bed, she rang the bank and told them that I wouldn't be in. I told her not to tell the truth about what had happened and we agreed that she would say that I'd fallen down the stairs and that nothing was broken but I needed to take it easy for a while.

As I heard her talking, to Anthony I think, I lay back on my pillows and all I could think was that I wouldn't be able to see Lucy that night and I had no way of letting her know.

It rained that Thursday night, the one after I'd been beaten, and I hoped that Lucy wasn't still standing in the street waiting for me to turn up. I looked at the clock and saw that it was an hour after the time we usually met and I took some comfort from the thought that surely she wouldn't have waited that long. She would be tucked up safely at home by then. Wouldn't she?

I wondered how long she would have waited for me. How long would I have waited for her? I suspect that I would have waited longer than she did.

LUCY

'Daniel said to say hello,' my father said the following evening.

'Did he?' I doubt he had because I knew for a fact that Daniel thought my father didn't know anything about our relationship. I nodded my head. 'Is he well?'

'He seemed fine but you know Daniel, he doesn't give much away,' he winked at me.

'How are things between you and Thomas?' my mother asked. She was sitting in her favourite spot on the sofa with what looked like a brandy in her hand and by the look on her face it wasn't her first glass.

'Fine,' I said.

'Should I be looking for a new outfit?' her eyes were starting to glaze over.

I looked at her. I knew what she was getting at but I didn't rise to the bait. 'I thought you were always on the look out for a new outfit, Mother,' I said coldly.

'You could do a lot worse,' her voice was just as cold.

'I'm sure I could,' I said the words slowly, 'but I'm in no hurry to become Mrs Wentworth.'

'Thomas is a very nice young man,' she drained her glass, 'and he has excellent prospects.'

'I don't need a man with excellent prospects,' I told her, 'I have perfectly good prospects of my own.'

As I left the room I passed my father who had buried his head into some papers that he was holding. He wasn't reading them; he was just trying to hide the smile on his face.

'Did you see my father?' I asked Daniel the following week. He looked a bit sheepish and said that he had. I asked him what they had talked about and he said it had just been business. My father had said that we had Daniel where we wanted him so I guessed that the meeting had been to put the final bits of our plan in place. He'd still not told me what that plan was, though I'd heard him talking about a new factory so I thought that it might have something to do with that. The thing is, if it *was* to do with the new factory, I couldn't really see why Daniel would be so important to my father. The name Arthur Braithwaite opens doors anywhere, so why Daniel?

I couldn't help thinking that things were going to get tricky. I don't mind tricky, it can be exciting.

Daniel and I continued to see each other once a week, on Thursdays for dinner and the occasional roll in a hotel room. I would have liked more of the rolling and less of the eating if I'm honest but you can't have everything.

At least Daniel seemed to have taken the hint about the type of places that I liked to eat and he always made reservations at good restaurants. We became quite the regulars at Le Petit Monde.

Thomas took me there one evening and I could see the double takes that the waiters gave us. It was just a brief moment and thank goodness Thomas didn't seem to notice. It was actually quite funny because a couple of weeks later when I turned up on Daniel's arm they did it again but he didn't notice either. Men really are quite dim sometimes.

Talking of Thomas, he was getting very keen. He just loved to buy me presents and of course I loved getting them. Oh come on, what girl wouldn't love getting presents? What was I supposed to do, tell him that I didn't want his jewellery and his chocolates? That would have been rude. The trouble was, he was expecting more from me which I still didn't enjoy because, well, frankly I don't even want to think about how it felt to have him on top of me. Maybe it wouldn't have been so bad if he just looked after himself a bit better but he didn't.

I know Daniel didn't have age on his side but he was still in good shape. Thomas was just soft and flabby by comparison. Thomas could have learned a thing or two from Daniel and while they were at it he could have told Thomas how to please a girl in bed.

Once, I turned up to my Thursday date with Daniel wearing a necklace that Thomas had bought me. Daniel commented on it and said how pretty it was and then the following week he turned up with a bracelet that was almost the same. At first glance you would have thought that they were matching. I was so grateful to him, a lot more than I had been when he'd given the necklace with the speck of sapphire dangling from it. The necklace

Thomas had bought wouldn't have even made a dent in his wallet but Daniel's poor little wifey had probably had her housekeeping cut to pay for the bracelet.

I continued to feel bad about Daniel's wife. Well I thought about her from time to time anyway.

So there wasn't really anything during the summer. I saw Thomas two or three times a week and Daniel on Thursdays and that was about all.

That was until the Thursday that I turned up at our usual meeting place and Daniel wasn't there. When Robert dropped me off I searched the bushes for some sign of Daniel hiding but I couldn't see him anywhere. I thought it was odd that he was late but when he hadn't turned up after an hour I knew that something was wrong.

It had even started to rain.

I called Robert and asked him to come back for me. I spent the fifteen minutes wondering what could have stopped Daniel from being there. Maybe his wife had finally cottoned on to what he was doing and had put her foot down. I couldn't see that though because there was no reason why she would find out. I could have believed it in the early days but not now. I couldn't imagine Daniel's wife had many friends that ate at Le Petit Monde or Poplar Lodge, so who would tell her? I thought that it was more likely that his conscience had got the better of him and he had decided to do the decent thing by the little woman at home.

I was soaking by the time Robert turned up.

'Everything alright Miss Lucy?' Robert asked as we drove away. I was taking one last look through the back window just in case Daniel had finally turned up, but there was no sign of him. Rain was dripping off my hair and down my face and I felt thoroughly miserable.

'Yes, everything's fine.'

My parents were having dinner with some friends of theirs that evening so the house was empty when I got home, which I was happy about. It was the first time in my life that I had been stood up and I didn't like it.

I hung my wet coat on the hook behind the door and didn't care what the drips might do to the carpet. I cared even less about what the rain would be doing to my hair and went straight to the drinks cabinet. I poured myself a drink that was more gin than orange. I would pay for it later but at that moment I didn't care. When my first drink was finished I poured myself another. By the time I went to bed I was drunk.

I lay on the bed and wondered why Daniel had stood me up. If he thought he could get rid of me that easily he would have another thing coming.

DANIEL

'I'm sorry you missed out on your night out,' Isobel said as she handed me a cup of cocoa. 'I know how much you look forward to your Thursday evenings.'

I risked burning my lips on the cocoa rather than say anything. How was I supposed to answer that one? She was right, I did look forward to my Thursday evenings, but not for the reasons that she thought.

'Never mind,' I was glad when she took the chance to carry on talking, 'I'm sure the world won't stop turning just because you didn't go to the club for one week.'

I hoped she was right.

Isobel went shopping on the Friday morning. She made sure I was settled in the armchair and gave me a cup of tea before she left. She said that she wouldn't be long.

I sat for a while, just thinking about things when I decided that I had to ring Lucy. I had to tell her why I hadn't been there the night before. I had Lucy's number – well I suppose it was her father's, really – written on a piece of paper that I kept hidden in the pocket of a coat I never wore. Once I was sure that Isobel was out I made my way to the bedroom and got that scrap of paper out of its hiding place.

I sat on the chair beside the table that the telephone sat on and dialled the numbers slowly.

It rang four or five times.

'Braithwaite residence,' the words *oh shit* went through my head as the voice said, 'this is Mrs Braithwaite speaking.' I didn't want to speak to Mrs Braithwaite. I opened my mouth but nothing came out. 'Hello, hello?' she said.

I coughed, 'I'm sorry,' I croaked, 'I think I have the wrong number.'

'Oh alright,' she sounded disappointed.

'Sorry.' I put the phone down and wondered what the hell I was doing.

I went back to work the following Monday. The bruises were more blue than black by then and at least most of them were covered by my suit. There was nothing that I could do about the ones on my face.

I hid myself in my office most of the day not even venturing out for lunch. I didn't think it would look good for customers to see me like that. Mrs Warren brought me about a dozen cups of tea throughout the day, and at lunchtime she brought me a sandwich that she had bought from the café on the corner. Apparently Mrs Holden had sent her love.

'I know you like it there,' she said, 'and as you said you weren't going out to lunch, I thought this might cheer you up.'

'How much do I owe you?' I asked but she waved it away.

'Bring me a custard tart back next time you go there,' she smiled at me, 'they looked lovely.'

I noticed that as well as the sandwich which was on a china plate, there were also two cups of tea on the tray that she had brought in. She set one of them in front of me and then rested the second on her lap as she sat in the chair opposite me.

I looked up from my sandwich. 'Mrs Warren?'

'It's been a while since we've done this,' she said. She watched me for a minute in that way that my mother used to when she had something that she wanted to say to me. 'Please tell me to mind my own business if you want,' she said, which made me laugh on the inside because that would be a total waste of time, 'but is everything alright?'

'Apart from the fact that I look like I've done a round or two with Rocky Marciano,' I tried to sound light hearted, 'I'm fine.'

'My brothers were both boxers,' she said, 'I've seen a lot of bruises in my time.' She said it as if she was just making a comment but I knew exactly what she was getting at. I couldn't bring myself to say anything. She emptied her tea and placed the cup and saucer on the tray. 'I'll leave you to enjoy your lunch,' she said. The door was open when she turned round and said, 'You're lucky Rocky Marciano doesn't live round here because if he'd done that you'd be dead.' She closed the door behind her.

She was the only one brave enough to mention my injuries, but I caught Johnson and Bridge giving me furtive glances and whispering in a corner. God knows what they

207

thought. Well, I know what they thought... the same as my secretary I dare say, and they would all be wondering who on earth was responsible. They realised I'd been given a beating but would have no idea who had done it. I knew that they would never guess.

The following Wednesday they – Jack's men – turned up again, but this time I was ready for them. When they met me on the street like they had the week before I was the one taking them round the corner out of sight.

'Danny,' it was the taller of the two that did the talking again, 'nice to see you. You're looking well.'

I wish I could have thought of something witty to say back to him but it was taking all I had just to keep everything together. I wouldn't like to tell you what my bowels were doing.

When I say 'the smaller of the two', it is just a relative term because despite being a few inches shorter than his colleague he was still massive. Well, the smaller of the two shuffled closer to me.

'So,' the taller one said, 'we're not going to have a problem here are we?'

I tried to say, 'No,' but it came out more like a squeak.

They laughed at me and I felt about six inches tall. 'What was that, Danny?'

I coughed to clear my throat. 'No,' I wanted to tell him that if he called me Danny one more time I'd knock his fucking head off but, wisely, I thought better of it.

As he held out his meaty hand I noticed that at least three fingers had rings on them. That explained the small darker bruises that still showed on my face. I reached into my inside pocket and pulled out a thick brown envelope. He made a point of moving his hand as if he was weighing it, trying to decide if it was as heavy as it should be. Then he lifted the flap and ran his thumb along the contents. He looked me square in the eye and I knew the question he was asking.

'It's all there,' I said.

He smiled widely, showing me the gaps at the back of his mouth where teeth used to be.

'Pleasure doing business with you, Danny,' he slapped me on the shoulder and nearly knocked me off my feet. 'See you next week.'

As they walked away I breathed properly for the first time in minutes.

I can see what you're thinking. You're wondering where I got the money from. Think about it. Dozens of people trust me to care for their money every day. They shouldn't have because I clearly couldn't be trusted.

Never in a million years would I have thought that I would steal from the people that I served. I know most of them personally. But it wasn't stealing really, it was just massaging figures. And it's not like I was going to keep it forever. The plan was that once I got myself back on my feet I would pay the money back and no-one would ever know that it had been missing in the first place.

I was cutting back financially on everything that I could. The housekeeping was, of course, untouchable. If I'd suddenly told Isobel that we had to start cutting back she would have known that there was something going on, but I was no longer saving anything at the end of the month and what we had put aside towards the house on Chestnut Avenue was long gone.

There were times when I wished that Isobel took more interest in our finances because then it wouldn't have been so easy to hide things from her, but as it was, it was the simplest thing in the world.

As I walked away from that encounter with Jack McGuire's henchmen I hated myself. I hated what I was doing and I hated the person I had become.

Isobel seemed surprised the following morning when I said that I would be going to my club as usual that evening.

'Are you sure you're up to it?' she asked as she dropped the breakfast dishes into the sink of soapy water. She picked a tea towel up and dried her hands. 'Your bruises still show.'

She was right, they did still show, I'd looked at them in the bathroom mirror just half an hour earlier. They were yellow by that time with a few dots of blue here and there.

'I'll be fine,' I said as I gathered my things and prepared to leave for work, 'it'll be dark so no-one will notice and even if they do, they are all too polite to say anything.'

As I walked along the street I couldn't help wondering if Lucy would even turn up.

I arrived at our meeting point at ten to seven and wasn't surprised that she wasn't there. Why would she be? I was early. By the time it was quarter past I started to think that she wasn't coming and the pit of my stomach felt like it was filled with lead.

Was this how it would end?

Maybe it wouldn't be such a bad thing. Maybe if it was over I would have a chance of getting my life back together. Things would return to how they had been. I'd get my finances back on the straight and narrow and everything would return to normal.

Did I want normal?

Well, it was a lot simpler than the life I was leading at the moment that was for sure. I didn't get beaten up when life was simple. I didn't steal money when life was simple.

But I didn't have Lucy when life was simple.

When I saw her coming round the corner I realised that I didn't want life to be simple.

She was scowling at me, like she was angry – which she had every right to be – but when she was close enough to see the bruising on my cheek her face softened into concern. She lifted her hand, the tips of her fingers barely brushing against my still-aching skin.

'What happened to you?' she asked.

'I fell down the stairs,' I said, but I could see the same look in her eyes that Mrs Warren had had when I'd tried to spin her that yarn. 'I did,' I took hold of her hand and kissed her finger tips. 'I did it last Wednesday and that's

211

why I wasn't here last week. I couldn't walk.' She still had a sceptical look on her face. 'I am so sorry that I couldn't come last week but I couldn't move. I barely got out of bed until Saturday morning.'

'I know,' she said.

'You know what?'

'That you fell down the stairs.'

I looked at her and asked, 'How did you know?'

'I went to the bank,' there was something in her eyes that I hadn't seen before. 'I went to the bank on Friday morning and your secretary told me that your wife had called to say that you had fallen down the stairs and wouldn't be in for a few days.'

I opened my mouth but nothing came out.

LUCY

I was still angry when I walked into the bank.

'Miss…' that drippy looking fella that sits at the front desk was flustered when he saw me.

'Braithwaite,' I snarled, 'the name you are looking for is Miss Braithwaite.'

'How can I help you, Miss Braithwaite?'

'I'm here to see Mr Laither.'

'I'm sorry, but that won't be possible,' he stammered.

I threw him a look full of the anger that I was feeling and I could see him shrink underneath it. I shouldn't laugh because it really was pitiful; it was like he got smaller as I looked at him. Without another word I brushed past him and made my way to Daniel's office. That man on the desk had probably been told to keep me out, but Daniel would need better security than that to stop me getting to him. I knew he was following me but there was no way he was going to stop me.

That woman, Daniel's secretary, was sitting at her desk typing when she caught sight of me heading her way.

'Miss Braithwaite,' she said as she pushed herself up from her desk and came towards me. 'Are you quite alright?'

Was she having a laugh? Did I look like I was alright?

I told her that I was there to see Mr Laither.

'I'm sorry but that won't be possible,' she said but I assumed she was saying exactly what she had been told to say.

'I'm sorry Mrs Warren,' the chap said it in an *I told her so* sort of way – I could have slapped him!

'That's alright Mr Johnson,' she said, 'I'll deal with this. You may go back to your desk.' Her head was held high in a manner that I suppose was meant to show that she was in charge of the situation. Her hands were joined in front of her chest and she smiled. Suddenly I felt like I was back in the headmistress' office at my last boarding school on the day that I was caught with a boy in my bedroom.

'I'm here to see Mr Laither,' I said again but even I could hear that there wasn't as much defiance in my voice anymore. 'If he is in a meeting, I'll wait.'

'That would be a waste of your time I'm afraid,' she said, 'Mr Laither isn't here.'

I looked at her trying to gauge if she was lying but I didn't think she was. 'Where is he?' I realised that I had no right to ask that sort of question so I tried to excuse it. 'I have a very important message from my father.'

'I can give him a message,' she picked up her pen and her pad.

'My father said that I was only to give it to Mr Laither.' I almost called him Daniel but I stopped myself just in time.

'Well I'm sorry,' she put the pad and pen down again, 'but I'm afraid Mr Laither is off sick today.'

'Sick?' It had never occurred to me that he might be ill. In a way, the fact that he was ill made me feel better because it meant that he hadn't stood me up.

'Yes, his wife said that he had fallen down the stairs.' I couldn't help feeling that Mrs Warren took delight in telling me that, you know, that his wife had called. She emphasised the word 'wife.' I could tell that she hadn't believed my story about a message from my father and maybe she had even guessed my real reason for being there. I'll bet she thought that she was telling me something that I didn't know.

As I walked away from the bank I thought about Daniel's wife. I wondered what she was like. How old was she? What did she look like?

I imagined someone about the same age as my mother but not so glamorous. I wouldn't like to think how much money my mother spends on make-up every week and I was fairly certain that Daniel's budget didn't run to that sort of thing, especially not since he'd started paying for meals at Le Petit Monde. I wondered if she had to do without things so that Daniel could fund our affair and part of me hoped that she hadn't but another part of me didn't give a damn.

If she had been the sort of wife that Daniel needed he wouldn't have come sniffing around me no matter how much I'd thrown myself at him.

When I woke up on the Thursday morning I lay in bed for a while and wondered about whether I should go to our meeting point that evening. Why should I? I was still angry about the week before. Could he not have phoned to tell me that he wouldn't be there? If he had phoned me I wouldn't have humiliated myself in front of his secretary.

I wanted to make someone pay and unfortunately for him, it would be Daniel.

I was late getting there but that was fine because I wanted him to feel just a little of what I had felt the week before. I wanted to give him a taste of his own medicine. You might think it's childish but I'm not going to apologise for it.

His eyes lit up when he saw me but I think it was with relief as much as anything.

My God, his face was a mess. The bruises were fading but they were still there. I could see that his lip had been cut but that was healed now apart from a red slit where the scab must have been.

I asked him what he had done and he told me he had fallen down the stairs. I didn't believe him and I was disappointed that he even tried that lie on me. Mrs bloody Warren might have fallen for it but I wasn't as gullible as her. I mean, why would his face be so bruised if he had fallen down the stairs and what sort of grown man just falls down the stairs?

When I told him that I knew because I had gone to the bank and his secretary had told me about his wife ringing, the little colour he had drained from his face. He opened his mouth but nothing came out.

I didn't have the same problem. I opened my mouth and the words, 'Daniel, I'm pregnant,' popped out.

DANIEL

'Pregnant?' the word came out like a squeal and I looked around to check that no-one had heard it. We were alone. 'Did you say you were pregnant?'

'Yes,' she said with a smile on her face. 'Isn't it marvellous?'

No it wasn't bloody marvellous and I couldn't imagine why she thought that it was. I wasn't in this relationship to have a baby and I was amazed that she thought it was anything other than an absolute disaster.

'What are you thinking Daniel?' There was something child-like in the way she spoke.

I remember running my hand over my head, pushing my hair back. I took off my glasses and wiped the back of my hand across my forehead. I thought I was going to be sick. 'Are you sure?' I asked.

'Yes,' she said, 'that's why I was late getting here. I had an appointment with the doctor this afternoon and he just told me.' She took hold of my face and forced me to look at her. 'What's wrong?'

What's wrong? What's wrong? What did she think was wrong? 'It's just a shock,' I said, which had to be the understatement of the decade.

'Poor you,' she brushed her fingers down the side of my face, 'I know this is an awful shock, it was for me too.'

I turned away and gave myself a second or two to get my thoughts together. When I turned back around she was still there, looking at me for an answer.

I didn't have any answers, I only had a question. 'What are you going to do?'

'Don't you mean what are *we* going to do, Daniel? It's your baby as much as it is mine.' I couldn't understand why she looked so happy. 'What do you think I'm going to do?' she asked, 'I'm going to have a baby.'

'But...' I have no idea what I was trying to say. My head was all over the place.

'But nothing Daniel,' She was smiling as she put my hand on her perfectly flat stomach. 'We are having a baby.'

We went to the nearest pub which happened to be The Red Lion in the market square and I ordered a couple of brandies. I didn't know about Lucy but I knew that I needed one, maybe more.

We sat at a table at the back and I drank mine down in one. Lucy sipped hers while I went back to the bar and ordered another.

'What are *we* going to do, Lucy?' I was careful choosing my words.

'What else can we do, silly? We'll have to get married.' I wondered for a second if I had heard her right. She knew about Isobel. She knew about my wife. She'd mentioned her earlier, hadn't she? It soon became clear that she didn't see that as a problem. She looked at me coyly and said, 'I know it's a bit difficult with you being married already but you won't be the first person to get divorced.'

I almost choked on the brandy I had just taken into my mouth and swallowed it quicker than I wanted to. 'You want me to ask Isobel to give me a divorce?'

'Yes,' she made it sound so simple.

I could feel myself shaking and I tried to force myself to take deep breaths just so that I could get a grasp of things. It's a good job that we were practically the only ones at the pub because God knows what I must have looked like.

'What's she like? Is she amenable?' Lucy asked in such a matter of fact sort of way that I wondered if she actually realised what it was that she was asking me to do. She was asking me to destroy another woman's life and she wasn't even batting an eyelid.

Who was this woman in front of me?

I asked myself if Isobel really would be destroyed and of course I knew that she would be. It would be bad enough for her to find out that I'd been sleeping with another woman, let alone a woman who was young enough to be my daughter and who was now carrying my child.

A baby of her own was the one thing that Isobel had wanted more than anything and it had been the one thing that I had never been able to give her. Month after month she'd cried when she realised that she still wasn't pregnant. I had held her as she wept and wondered what was wrong with me. There was no relief in knowing that it wasn't my fault after all. Maybe she could have forgiven me for the affair, but not for giving another woman a child.

And then to ask for a divorce, she wouldn't be able to bear the shame, and why should she? She had done nothing wrong.

I could hardly face her when I went home. There she was, all 'Did you have a nice evening?' and 'Did you meet anyone interesting?' and all the while I'm thinking what the hell am I going to do?

She said that she thought I looked peaky and I thought *is it any bloody wonder?*

She didn't deserve this, any of it. I know we'd sort of fallen into marriage but our vows had meant something to her and she had always been a good wife. She was a good woman and I didn't think that I could do it to her.

I spent every waking moment thinking about it and given that I didn't sleep a lot that meant that there was a lot of time to think.

I did come up with one thought though, and I wasn't proud of that either.

The following Thursday I went to meet Lucy as usual and I hoped, no I prayed that she would tell me that there wasn't a baby any more. Not fathering a child was my only regret prior to what was going on with Lucy but I could have lived with that. I had lived with it long enough already.

I hadn't made dinner reservations anywhere but she said that she was starving so we went to a restaurant on Silver Street, the one near the bakers. I wasn't very hungry to start with but when Lucy whispered to me that she could eat a horse because she was eating for two I lost the little appetite I'd had. She ordered steak, mashed potatoes and vegetables and I had vegetable soup though I defy anyone to tell me what those vegetables were. To be fair it was probably very good but all I could taste was the bile that had sat in my mouth all week.

'How are you?' I asked. It seemed like the polite thing to do.

'Sick in the mornings but apart from that I feel fine. I think my mother might suspect something though because she asked me yesterday if there was anything that I wanted to tell her.' She cut off a slice of steak and smiled at me as she chewed.

'Lucy,' I said slowly as I went over in my head for the millionth time the thing that had dominated my thoughts for the last few days. 'I've been thinking,' I paused here to give myself a few more seconds, 'and the thing is, I don't think I can do it.'

'Do what?' she asked as she swallowed.

I blurted the words out as quickly as I could. I just needed to get them said; 'I don't think I can ask Isobel for a divorce.'

The sound of her knife and fork clashing onto her plate echoed through the room and a couple of people turned. A waiter who had been taking an order at a nearby table turned to ask if everything was alright. I assured him that it was even though it clearly wasn't.

I watched Lucy who was deliberately looking at her plate; I could see from the rise and fall of her chest that she was taking deep breaths. Eventually she lifted her head and looked at me.

'And why not?' she asked. If I'm honest she scared me a bit. There was something in her eyes that told me I had said the wrong thing.

I reached across the table and tried to take her hand but she pulled it away from me. She raised an eyebrow to show me that she expected an answer to her question.

'Look, Lucy,' I said, 'if I was free then I would marry you without a second thought, but I'm not free and Isobel doesn't deserve to be hurt by what we've been doing.'

'It's a pity you didn't worry about that before, isn't it Daniel?' she was almost spitting the words at me. 'It's a pity you didn't think about her when you were groaning underneath me in bed.' Why did she have to be so coarse? I couldn't keep looking at her. 'I don't recall you calling her name when you were taking your pleasure from me. In fact,' she laughed, 'I don't remember you even mentioning her at all.'

'I…' I opened my mouth but couldn't find any words to justify myself. There weren't any. Lucy was right. 'I'm sorry,' I said, though it didn't seem adequate.

'Sorry is no good to me, Daniel,' she plucked up her knife and fork again and cut off another piece of steak. 'I'm having your baby and I need your support.' She smiled and spoke in the sweetest of voices which made it all the more sinister.

It didn't matter what I said, she wouldn't be moved. She had this notion in her head that Isobel would agree to divorce me just because I asked her to.

'Why wouldn't she?' Lucy asked. 'When you tell her about us she'll be so incensed by your disloyalty that she'll want rid of you anyway. She'll not know how quick to get herself a solicitor and file for divorce.'

She really didn't know the first thing about Isobel or how she would react. But then, why would she? She didn't know her at all. Isobel had been my secret and I was devastated that she hadn't stayed that way.

'She'll be annoyed I'm sure,' I said, 'and she'll be hurt beyond words but she is an honourable woman. She took her wedding vows for life, for better and for worse.'

'Even if you tell her that you've been sleeping with someone else?' she scoffed.

'She would rather suffer the embarrassment of that than the shame of a divorce.' They weren't just words that I hoped would get me out of the mess I was in, it was the truth. Divorce would be Isobel's worst nightmare.

'Well then my love, you have a problem.' Lucy had finished her meal and wiped her mouth with her napkin. How could she eat? I'd hardly touched my soup so that would be three bob down the drain. For the first time in our relationship I felt nothing when she smiled at me.

I didn't know what else to do so I asked my friend Stephen for advice the following day. Have I mentioned that he's a solicitor? I told him that I was asking for a friend.

'He's got himself into a fix,' I told him. 'He's been seeing another woman and he wants to divorce his wife so that he can marry her.'

We'd met for our usual Friday night pint after work and were sitting in the snug at The Golden Fleece. It's on my way home and close to Stephen's office so it made sense.

Stephen thought for a moment or two, the way he always does, before asking if my 'friend' had retained professional help yet.

'I don't think so,' I said, 'we were just chatting and I told him that I had a friend who was a solicitor and he asked me if I would have a word with you. You don't mind do you?'

'Of course not,' Stephen licked the froth that had formed a moustache on his upper lip, 'but I would advise that he gets himself a solicitor if he is serious about this.'

'I'll tell him,' I kept sipping at me beer, trying to appear that everything was normal. 'But just so I can tell him, will it be hard for him to get a divorce?'

He said that it might be messy but not impossible. His wife would be able to file for divorce on the grounds of his adultery. I was just starting to think that maybe things wouldn't be so bad when he dropped a bombshell. 'There will be a court case though and your friend's mistress will be named as co-respondent.'

The beer I'd just swallowed reappeared in the back of my throat and I gagged.

LUCY

I hadn't planned on telling Daniel that I was pregnant, the words were just out of my mouth before I realised it. However, once I had said it I was glad that I had.

I was just so angry with him. I was angry that he hadn't rung me the week before to say he wouldn't be coming and I didn't believe for a second that he'd been in bed until Saturday morning. I didn't believe that he'd fallen down the stairs either. I was angry that he was lying to me. I was angry and hurt and I wanted him to hurt too.

Oh you should have seen the colour drain from his face when I told him about the baby. I thought he was going to faint. I was glad that there wasn't really a baby because it was the last thing that I wanted and it appeared that Daniel felt the same way.

I was pleased that he felt that way because it meant that I would be able to hurt him. I might even be able to have a little fun doing it.

We went to some filthy back street pub and he bought two double brandies. Oddly enough, to say it was a hell hole of a place they did serve a very good brandy. Do you like a good brandy? I do.

He asked me what we were going to do. He sounded a bit pathetic if I'm honest. I've learnt this trick from my father. When I'm pretending to be something I'm not, like when I'm supposed to be in love with someone but really all I want is for him to give me something that he doesn't want to be parted from, I take on the role of the person I'm supposed to be. I become that person. Do you know what I mean? My father says that all the best actresses use that method. I think I would make a marvellous actress.

So in my head I became someone who was pregnant by a married man. I behaved the way that I thought I would if I really were in that position.

I'd told my father about Daniel not turning up for our evening together the week before but I hadn't told him that I'd been to the bank and what Daniel's secretary had told me. I couldn't have done that without him seeing how angry the secretary had made me and he's always telling me that my temper will get me into trouble. So the morning after I had seen Daniel's bruises for myself I took my father to one side and said, 'I saw Daniel last night.'

'Did you?' he said as he collected his things together and put them in his briefcase. 'How was he?'

I told him about the state of his face. 'Apparently he fell down the stairs at home,' I said.

'That was very clumsy of him,' my father chuckled.

He started telling me a story of how one day, after he'd taken a beating from someone that he owed money to he'd told his mum that he'd fallen down the stairs. 'She believed me of course because she wanted to,' Dad said, still laughing at the recollection, 'but anyone who wanted to see what was really going on knew. Two totally different types of bruises you see. Anyway, who ever got a bruised face from falling down the stairs? Interesting,' he started to nod his head, 'I wonder what young Danny's been up to?' I couldn't help thinking that he knew more than he was letting on.

I didn't tell him that I had told Daniel I was pregnant.

Later, when I was on my own, I started to think about what my father had said. It was obvious to anyone who knew what to look for that Daniel had been given a beating. What I didn't understand was why anyone would want to beat Daniel to a pulp. Why does any man get a beating?

I've seen it happen to a man that was having an affair with a married woman. Her husband had caught wind of it and left him with two black eyes and a broken nose. Well I wasn't married and I somehow didn't see Thomas doing that sort of thing even if he'd had an inkling of what was going on between Daniel and me. I had always been very careful in that regard.

The only other reason I could think of was what my father had said. You might be beaten if you owed money to someone and then didn't pay them pack. I'm not talking about a bank loan because I'm sure they don't resort to that kind of thing if you miss a payment, I mean… what do you call them…? Loan sharks, I think that's what they're called. You know the ones I mean, people that lend money to those that are desperate.

That didn't seem plausible either. I know Daniel had been spending a lot of money on me but I couldn't imagine him owing money to one of those people. I mean he's a bank manager for goodness sake, he knows how to manage money, and anyway, if he needed money wouldn't he just get a bank loan? I've heard you get really good deals on loans and things if you work for a bank. That's what my friend Lizzie said anyway, though I'm not sure how she knows.

I was pleased to see him the following Thursday because I'd had my doubts that he'd turn up. I wondered if I had misjudged the hold I had over him and pushed him too far. I thought that maybe he would try to distance himself from me and the tiny little problem that he thought we had but that feeling didn't last long because that's just not the sort of thing that Daniel would do. He is an honourable man. Plus he wouldn't dare.

He hadn't booked anywhere for dinner which disappointed me a bit because I thought that, especially now, I deserved to be treated well. Instead of a lovely restaurant we ended up going to a place on Silver Street for something to eat. I don't remember what it's called but I don't suppose that matters. It was next door to a butcher's shop I think, or was it a baker's? I didn't really notice if I'm honest.

I had steak, mashed potatoes and vegetables as I recall, and I think Daniel had soup. He said he wasn't hungry. I wasn't that hungry either but I made a thing about needing to eat for two. He went a very odd colour when I said that, almost the colour of frog spawn. It didn't suit him at all.

I was actually starting to feel sorry for him and I almost considered coming up with a way of making the baby go away. That was until he told me that he hadn't told his wife that he wanted a divorce. No, what he actually said was that he didn't think that he could ask her for a divorce. He said something about how he wouldn't think twice about marrying me if he was free but he wasn't and he was sorry. That was easy to say.

Did he honestly think that 'Sorry,' would cut the mustard? He obviously didn't know me very well.

He said that his wife was a good woman and that she didn't deserve to be hurt. Well I'm sure she was but that wasn't really my problem was it. I reminded him that he hadn't been thinking about what a wonderful woman she was while he was with me. Well it's true. He'd never even mentioned her. Daniel hadn't even thought that she was worth mentioning. He was the one that had played away, not me. You can't count Thomas.

I was just thinking about what was best for my baby. My baby was the most important thing to me. My baby needed its father. I know it might sound odd but sometimes I actually felt like my imaginary baby was real.

I really didn't think that I was asking too much.

I know that if I had a husband who came home one day and said that he had been having an affair with someone and that that someone was pregnant I'd definitely want a divorce. But for some reason Daniel thought that his wife would be different. Well in my mind that just made her an idiot. He went on about her not wanting the shame of a divorce but for goodness sake I thought that was ridiculous. To me a divorce is nothing compared to the shame of everyone knowing that your husband has fathered a child with another woman, and trust me, if I really had been pregnant and she hadn't agreed to the divorce I would make sure that everyone within fifty miles knew that I was having her husband's baby.

I made it clear that I expected him to tell his wife that he wanted a divorce. Why would he ask her? He's a man and he needed to start acting like one.

I think that was the night I lost any respect for him and, to be honest, I hadn't had that much to start with. I mean, what sort of man would turn his back on his pregnant girlfriend because he didn't want to upset his wife by divorcing her.

He was pathetic.

DANIEL

I'd spent much of the following days in a trance. My body was there, at home and in the office, going through the motions, but my head wasn't. I couldn't concentrate on anything.

By two o'clock on Wednesday I'd had enough. I told Mrs Warren I was feeling ill and needed to go home and asked her to get Bridge to take my afternoon appointments. There were only a couple and nothing he couldn't handle so I didn't think anyone would miss me.

I was packing my things into my briefcase when I heard the phone in the outer office ring and Mrs Warren answered it with her usual efficiency. I had just come out of my office when I heard her say, 'If you'll just wait a moment Mr Braithwaite I'll check if he is still here. He has a dental appointment this afternoon I believe.' She was looking at me for instruction and I shook my head vigorously. Arthur Braithwaite was the last person I wanted to speak to and I rue the day I had ever heard his name. 'I'm sorry Mr Braithwaite,' she said politely, 'it would appear that he has already left. Could Mr Bridge help you with anything?' I watched her as she listened to his response. 'May I give him a message?' again she listened. 'Thank you, goodbye.' She put the phone back on its cradle.

'Thank you,' I said as I finally dared to move and close the door behind me.

'I hope you're feeling better soon,' she said but when I looked at her she had already gone back to her typing.

Despite the familiarity we shared I had always felt that there had been a respect of my position as her boss but when I looked at her now I had a feeling that all that was gone.

I went to the park and sat on a bench. There weren't many people around, not at that time on a midweek afternoon, and those that were weren't close enough to disturb me.

I suppose the top and bottom of it is that I'm a coward and the thought of confessing to Isobel terrified me. How could I possibly tell her that I had made a sham of everything that we had been through over the last decade and a half?

Not only had I betrayed her, I had ruined us financially and I wasn't sure which would upset her the most. Isobel had set her heart on a house on Chestnut Avenue but there was no chance of that now. I had used up the savings, my salary didn't cover our outgoings, and I was fiddling the books at the bank to cover up the fact that I was siphoning off money to pay a loan shark. And if that wasn't bad enough, Lucy was pregnant.

As I sat there, mulling things over and feeling sicker by the minute I realised that I only had one option.

Marrying Lucy would solve all my problems. I mean, I know I'd be over a barrel to her father but he wouldn't see his beloved daughter go without. He'd make the money problems go away and who knows, maybe I could persuade him, over time, to help Isobel out, you know, in light of her being so understanding. I realised by then that it was just a matter of time before what I was doing at the bank was uncovered. I'd already had to dip into bank funds twice just so that I could pay Jack and I couldn't see any other way to pay my debts. Lucy's father wouldn't see her married to a jailbird so I was fairly certain he would grease a few palms and the mess would go away. I had a feeling he would remind me of it every chance he got but that was just the price that I was going to have to pay.

I knew what I had to do and I started the journey home as if I was carrying the world on my back.

Isobel stared at me like she couldn't believe what I was saying to her, though I'm not sure why she would think that I was making it up.

She had been in the dining room setting the table when I got home and had come into the hallway when she'd heard me come through the door. She smiled and said that dinner would be just a couple of minutes. I said that dinner could wait because I needed to talk to her.

'What about?' she asked but I didn't answer her.

I followed her into the kitchen and watched as she took a pie from the oven and turned the light off under a saucepan.

She turned to face me and her forehead creased as she looked at me. 'What's wrong Daniel?' she asked.

There was nothing for it but to spit it out. There was no easy way to say it so I said it quick. 'I want a divorce.'

'What?' her voice rose to almost a squeak and she leaned back against the wall like she was about to fall down. 'Daniel, what do you mean?'

I could feel myself shaking as I said it again. 'I want a divorce.' I could hear it in my voice too.

She was opening and closing her mouth but I think she was gasping for air rather than trying to speak. She looked at me as if she was trying to work out if I was telling the truth or just having some sort of sick joke. She got her answer from the look on my face. Eventually she managed to say one word. 'Why?'

I weighed up in my head how much I should tell her and decided that the only thing to do was to tell her the whole truth and throw myself on her mercy.

First of all I apologised over and over for what I had done. I told her that none of this was her fault and that I was completely to blame. I told her that Lucy had caught me in a moment of weakness and that I had never meant for it to happen but somehow it had and things had got out of control. I didn't tell her all the gory details of the financial nightmare but I did tell her that the savings were gone. The words hit her like a thump in the stomach and she doubled over. I moved an inch or two towards her but she screamed at me to get away.

I watched her shoulders rise and fall as she struggled to control her breathing. There was nothing that I could do to help her so I watched and waited. I was just starting to worry that she might be having a heart attack when she used her hands on her knees to push herself upright.

'What if I forgive you?' her voice was only just above a whisper, 'we don't have to move,' her eyes flicked around the room. 'We've been happy here, we could be happy again.'

There was something pathetic about her standing there with tears in her eyes almost begging me to change my mind despite everything that I had told her.

'I want to marry her,' I've never hated myself more than I did when I said that.

Her eyes were wide and a little bit wild as they moved around like she was searching for the words she needed. 'You're married to me,' she said.

'I have to marry her,' I realised that I was going to have to tell her the whole truth. 'I have to marry her because she's pregnant.'

The pitiful look that had been in her eyes was replaced by something else, something dark, something that scared me.

'Pregnant?' somehow she made a whisper sound like a scream. 'You have made your tart pregnant? How did you manage that? You've fired blanks for the last fifteen years.' Isobel is the most ladylike woman I have ever met and her words plus the way that she was screaming at me made her seem like someone other than herself.

'I never meant for you to get hurt,' I told her but the words sounded hollow.

She threw her head back as she laughed. It was loud and bordering on hysterical. 'Then why did you do it, Danny?' She had never called me Danny before but now she seemed to delight in it. 'Come on,' she goaded, 'tell me Danny, why did you do it?'

'I don't know,' I said, 'it just happened.' I knew it was no answer but it was the only one that I had.

'Just happened? Just happened,' she had crossed the border to total hysteria by this point and her eyes were almost bulging out of her head. 'Having an affair with someone doesn't just happen. Making them pregnant doesn't just happen. You chose to do both. But the best of it is you want me to give you a divorce so that you can marry her. Are you stupid? Why would I do that? I haven't done anything wrong.'

'You're right, you haven't done anything wrong,' I tried to sound apologetic, 'but she's pregnant.'

'Then she's going to have a bastard.' She leaned forward with a mad look in her eyes as she spat the words at me.

'Come on Isobel; don't be like this, the baby hasn't done anything wrong. It deserves to be born in wedlock.' I hoped that making it sound like she was doing the baby a favour would appeal to her better nature. It didn't.

'Then it's having a bit of bad luck isn't it, Danny? Because I'm not going to agree to it.'

I know that I didn't really have the right to, but I was starting to lose my temper with her. She just wasn't ready to see reason. 'You do realise that I can still divorce you, don't you?' I said.

'Not in time to marry your whore before your brat is born,' she laughed, 'and not without her being named in court.' I wondered how she knew that but she was quick to explain. 'Did you think that I wouldn't get to hear about the little chat that you had with Stephen? That's the thing about having a happy marriage, you see – they talk to each other, and Sylvia talks to me.' She banged her hand against her forehead, 'And I thought you were talking about Johnson. How could I have been so stupid?'

We stood in the kitchen looking at each other. I could feel the muscles in my face twitching and so were hers.

'Who is she?' she asked.

'It doesn't matter,' I said, but she told me that it did. I succumbed and said, 'Her name is Lucy.'

'Lucy,' she mocked. 'You don't get many of them round here.'

I said the wrong thing when I said. 'I'm sure her father will make sure you are well compensated.'

'Will he now? Rich is he, this Lucy's dad?'

'He's Arthur Braithwaite.' That took the wind out of her sails. Her eyes widened and her breathing deepened. I saw that as my moment, I thought I had her. 'I'm sure he will make you very comfortably off,' I told her. I wasn't, but to my shame I wasn't that bothered. I could see the movement

238

behind her eyes as she thought about what I had just told her but I wasn't prepared for her answer.

'No,' her voice was calm and clear.

My teeth were clenched together and I had to prise them apart to speak. 'Why?'

'Because I don't want to,' her lips smiled but her eyes were sneering at me as she added, 'Danny.' She watched me, looking for some reaction I suppose. She pushed herself away from the counter she had been leaning on and started to slowly pace around the kitchen. After half a dozen steps she was standing in front of me. Her face was only a couple of inches from mine, close enough for me to feel her breath on my face as she spoke. 'And there's nothing you, Lucy, or Mr Arthur Braithwaite can do about that.' Again she paused for effect before adding that word, 'Danny.'

I hadn't even realised that there was a knife beside me and certainly didn't know it was in my hand until I felt the blood running down my wrist.

LUCY

I got the shock of my life when I got the phone call telling me about what had happened. When I last spoke to Daniel I had no idea that he was thinking about doing anything like that. Don't you think I would have telephoned the police if I'd thought he was going to do something as stupid as that? Of course I would.

My father is a great friend of the Chief Constable. He came to our house on New Year's Eve. I danced with him. If I'd known what Daniel was planning I'd have reported it straight away. That poor woman.

I know people are saying that I'm to blame, that I pushed him too far by telling that I was having a baby but I just wanted to hurt him, that was all. He'd hurt me and I wanted to hurt him back.

None of this is my fault.

ARTHUR BRAITHWAITE

I'm not going to pretend I'm something I'm not. I haven't always played by the rules and if I can use someone's weakness to my advantage I will.

Did I use Bill Morris? Some people will say that I did but let me tell you something, I wasn't the one that came up with the idea of a cheap loan. I barely knew him. I think I'd only met him twice before the day he called me out of the blue and asked if he could come to see me. He said that he had a proposition that he thought I'd be interested in.

I'm not sure of his reasons behind what he was doing and I didn't ask. People do that a lot you know, try to ingratiate themselves with me. I have a lot of influence and I suppose he thought if he did me a favour I'd owe him one back at some time in the future. It's just the way business works. I've no doubt he thought he'd get something out of it, but I don't know what. He certainly didn't get anything from me unless you count the Christmas card we sent.

He came to my office at the end of last October and said that he'd heard I was planning a new factory. It's common knowledge so I didn't mind him knowing but I asked him what that had to do with him. He asked if the funding was in place and, given that I knew his line of business I said that I was still open to options.

He said that I could get a good rate from his bank and I told him that a good rate didn't interest me. I could get a good rate anywhere. What I needed was a great rate. I mean, he was asking me to move away from a bank that I had used for years. He sweated a bit and eventually came up with an interest rate that was a good deal less than what is normally offered. Well, I know I've got a lot of money and the reason for that is that I'm careful and a cheap loan is not something to be sniffed at.

I said he had a deal as long as it was done quickly. I didn't want him changing his mind, though I doubt he'd have been brave enough to tell me if he had. I thought he'd suggest the one on High Street because that's their flagship branch so when he suggested a poxy back-street branch I knew that this was something old Billy boy was keeping secret from the men at the top. That didn't matter to me, I didn't care as long as I got my money and I had the right paperwork there was nothing that they could do… to me anyway… and I didn't really care what they did to Bill.

So it was Danny Laither that he sent to do his dirty work. And before I'd even met him I knew he'd be pliable. He'd have to be, you see, because Bill had managed to get him to do something that he knew he shouldn't have been doing. Then I thought, maybe he's not pliable, maybe he owed Bill or maybe he had been offered something. I didn't really care which of them he was because all of them made him weak.

I can do something with weak.

I've told you all this so that you can see that the deal I did with Danny was a legitimate business agreement and that I wasn't the one bending the rules.

I didn't plan that original meeting between Danny and Lucy. I'd asked Lucy to come to my office but I thought that the meeting would have been over by then. She came breezing into my office just as we were finishing up.

I introduced her to Danny just like I would introduce her to anyone she met in my office. She is my only child and one day everything I have will be hers so it's important that she meets people that are involved in the business. I'm starting to teach her the ropes so that when I'm gone what I've built up over the years will be in safe hands.

I took Daniel to lunch at Poplar Lodge. Part of it was as a thank you for facilitating the loan but I can't lie to you, I had seen the way that Daniel had looked at Lucy when they'd met in my office and I knew that we could use her to keep him sweet, keep him on side if you will. I told Lucy to 'drop by' in time for dessert.

Poplar Lodge is all well and good for impressing people, but the food's a bit ponsy for me. I left them having some of that foreign stuff that Lucy loves and I stopped off at the bakers on Victoria Road and bought a cream horn which I took back to the office and had with a cup of tea.

Despite what you might have heard I'm a simple man at heart.

Look, I'm her father and I don't want to know about some of the things that my daughter does but I know that they spent the afternoon together.

What I need you to know is that although I told her to keep him sweet, I never told Lucy to have that sort of relationship with Danny, and I certainly never told her to sleep with him.

Do I look like a pimp?

I knew that Danny was married, and Lucy knew he was, but let's be honest, Danny knew it better than any of us and he didn't seem to be bothered by it. I'm not going to condemn him for it because I've had the odd extra marital dalliance myself. All I was interested in was that Lucy didn't get hurt and I made that clear to him on the odd occasion that we met. Not in so many words because I didn't know for sure that he was having it off on the sly with my daughter but I think he got the message.

I'm going to say Lucy's real boyfriend was a bloke called Tommy Wentworth whose father is a flash git that was born into money so doesn't know what it is to do a day's work. Tommy is supposed to have a job but it's not one I've ever heard of. I call Tommy Lucy's real boyfriend because I'm sure Danny was nothing more than a bit of rough.

In a way I felt sorry for Danny because Tommy could buy Lucy beautiful presents and take her to the best places. Do you know he drives a Bentley? Danny goes to work on the bus. How was he supposed to compete with that?

Well it became clear to me that Danny was at least trying because one day one of the people that runs one of my sidelines came to see me.

I lend money to people who can't get it from the bank. Some people would call the likes of me loan sharks but really we are just offering a service and, like any service, it has to be paid for. I learnt that Danny was taking advantage of that service. I can't be seen doing it myself so I use a man called Jack McGuire to take care of that little enterprise. I have always made it clear that I want to know if someone isn't making their payments so he came to me about six or seven weeks ago and told me that someone wasn't paying what they owed and did I want him to turn up the heat. They were his words not mine. I think he's been watching too many gangster films. Anyway, he said that he'd already sent 'the boys' round with a warning and he wanted me to authorise them taking the next step should he renege on his obligations once again. I told him to stop pussy-footing around and, if need be, of course he should let 'the boys' do what they do best.

'Who is it anyway?' I asked just before he left my office.

'A bloke who used to be in our kids class at school,' he said. 'He's called Daniel Laither.' He rubbed his nose to try and hide his smile. 'Guess what? He's a bank manager.'

I smiled too. So this was how he was financing his affair.

When Lucy came home and said that Daniel had allegedly fallen down the stairs I knew that he had failed to make his loan repayment again.

Do you know what the ironic thing is? I'd never actually needed to borrow money for the factory so the money I borrowed at next to no interest I lent out at a much greater rate. I've earned a fortune off it. Danny was borrowing the money that he had lent to me in the first place.

That was a few weeks ago and then the next thing I know, you ring and say there's been a stabbing and that you want to talk to me.

Who's stabbed who anyway? And what's it got to do with me or my daughter?

DEARDON

I've been a police officer around here for over forty years. When I first met Arthur Braithwaite I was a constable on my first day on the job and he was a mouthy seventeen year old who had stolen his mother's purse.

His mother had reported the purse missing a couple of days earlier, saying that she had had it when she was at the butchers shop only to discover it was missing a couple of hours later. She thought it had been nicked from her shopping bag while she was out. The station sergeant, a bloke called Frank Bradley, suggested I go with him on a visit to Connie Braithwaite's house.

It took me less than five minutes to see through Arthur Braithwaite's story but Frank's experience meant that he was a couple of minutes quicker. The lad denied he'd stolen the purse and said that his mother had given it to him so that that he could get the money he needed out of it.

'You're getting forgetful in your old age Ma,' he had said with a grin on his face. 'You gave it me and told me to take what I wanted.' He had kept a cigarette hanging from the corner of his mouth the whole time he was talking.

I think she realised that she hadn't forgotten anything of the sort but she said that she had. I was the one looking into her eyes and I could see what she was thinking as clear as day. She knew full well that her son had stolen her purse and every penny that was in it.

247

Arthur Braithwaite was a liar then and he's a liar now.

He sat in front of me today and said that he didn't know why William Morris had offered to get him a cheap loan but I don't believe that for a second. I know why he did it and Arthur does too.

It was desperation.

William Morris was a desperate man and desperate men do desperate things. Arthur Braithwaite will never convince me that he didn't know just how desperate Morris was because he makes it his business to know everything that's going on in this town. After old Bill Morris died it took us less than half an hour to work out why he was desperate and I'd bet my pension that Arthur knew before we did.

Arthur Braithwaite went off to France in 1915 and although I never heard her say it in so many words, I think Connie hoped that her son would come back a changed man. I can think of at least half a dozen people who hoped he didn't come back at all. In the end none of them got their wish, and when he walked back into town in 1918 he was just as he had always been – maybe even a bit worse.

Have you heard the rumours about how he got the money to set himself up in business? You might have heard the one about it being a big win on the horses or that he had a long-lost rich uncle but neither of those things are true. Let me enlighten you.

He blackmailed his father.

It was around 1920 when he asked his mother about Charles Matthews.

For a long time I thought this was just folk lore, something more interesting than what really happened, but now I know the truth. The Chief Constable at the time was a man called George Henry Macdonald and he was a personal friend of Charles Matthews. G H, as he was known to his friends, had heard the blackmail story straight from the horse's mouth, as it were, so that's how I know it to be true. Before G H retired about fifteen years ago he told the story to a few of us. He'd also told us all to keep a close eye on 'that bastard Braithwaite.' He told us that he had tried to persuade his friend to press charges but Matthew's wouldn't hear of it. He'd told G H that there had been an affair with a maid some years before which had resulted in the low life that we now know as Arthur Braithwaite. When it had been discovered that the maid was pregnant she left the house immediately and, with the understanding that his part in Arthur's birth remain a secret forever, Charles had supported Connie and her child. He had even found a job for his illegitimate son after the war.

We've never known who told Arthur that the man he called 'boss' was also his father but that was Charles Matthews' worst nightmare come true. He had kept his indiscretion a secret for more than twenty years before the day that Arthur walked into his office and said either Charles pay him what he wanted or he would introduce himself to Vanessa Matthews and share his news with her.

G H said that he didn't know his friend's reasons for paying up or why he had refused to let us charge his son with the crime he had committed but whatever his reasons,

Charles gave Arthur what he asked for. I've never heard exactly how much money Arthur got from his father but it was substantial enough him to set himself with a business and buy his own factory.

Since then he has built an empire and I'm willing to bet that someone else has paid the price for every step that he has taken.

William Morris was just one of those steps.

We'll never know what made William choose Daniel to facilitate the loan he had set up for Arthur but I suspect it was that he knew Daniel was ambitious. Daniel has told me that it was implied that the High Street branch could be his and perhaps William knew that was all it would take.

I hope you don't believe for a second that Arthur didn't know what his daughter was doing with Daniel. Maybe he told the truth when he said that he didn't say it in so many words but it wouldn't have surprised me if he had. I don't think Lucy realises that her father was using her too. He told me that he wasn't a pimp but I suggest that that is exactly what he was in this case. He said that he told her that she was to keep Daniel happy but I am under no illusion that Lucy only did what was expected of her.

Once Arthur found out that Daniel was married he would have known the best way to manipulate his new financial friend. Lucy was his secret weapon and she played her part to perfection.

To my way of thinking, she played her part a bit too well for this to have been the first time they had used this particular ploy and the thought of that makes me sick to my stomach. How many other men have fallen foul of them before?

Mind, from what I hear Lucy's slept with most of the men under forty in this town whether her father wanted to use them or not. I know Daniel was a bit older than that but I doubt she'd have taken much persuasion. From the look in her eyes she would have slept with me if she thought it would help her out. She'd have been wasting her time though because I'm too long in the tooth to start messing around with tarts like her.

We've had our suspicions about Arthur's money-lending sideline for a while but never been able to prove anything. He's a low-life and I'd like to see him put away for it, not that it's going to happen. It's no secret that he has the new Chief Constable in his pocket.

Until I actually spoke to Arthur I believed that this had been about financing a factory on the cheap, but from Arthur's own mouth we now know that it was just an opportunity to make more money off the misery of others.

The man disgusts me.

I've known Lucy Braithwaite all of her life, not personally of course but as the child of someone that we kept an eye on.

There are two words that describe Lucy Braithwaite to perfection. Spoiled brat.

From the day that she was born she has been given everything that she wanted. Whatever she asked for she got.

I suppose we shouldn't be surprised that she turned out the way that she did.

Having said that, she knew that what she was doing was wrong. She knew that Daniel was married though she admits that it wouldn't have made any difference to her, and she also knew that her father was using him. She had encouraged Daniel to buy her things and take her to places that he couldn't afford and she blatantly played him off against a much richer man knowing full well that he could never compete but would ruin himself trying. She had used him every bit as much as her father had.

But let us remember that she wasn't just using him for baubles and food. She was using him for her own physical pleasure. I've already told you that I think her father acted like a pimp so I suppose what I'm saying is that Lucy acted like a whore.

She has said that none of this was her fault but I beg to differ.

It was spite that made her tell Daniel that she was pregnant. Spite and annoyance because he hadn't called her to say that he couldn't make one of their evenings out. I don't know why him standing her up would make her tell him that she was having a baby but that was apparently the reason that she did. She'd wanted to get back at him. Maybe you'd have to be a woman to understand her logic or perhaps she was just trying to justify her actions.

I don't think anything could justify them.

If she hadn't told Daniel that she was pregnant and then forced him to feel like he had no option than to ask Isobel for a divorce then what happened in that kitchen yesterday would never have happened.

Lucy has to take responsibility of that.

The thing I really don't get is his problem with being called Danny. I've got an Uncle Danny and you couldn't wish to meet a better bloke. My given name is John but lots of people have called me Johnny over the years and it's never bothered me and my brother has never been called Albert since the day he was born apart from on official forms and by our mam when he'd done something wrong. Daniel blames his mother for him not liking the name Danny but I don't buy that. Blaming your mother for something like that is just a cop out. She might have always called him by his full name but that doesn't make any of this her fault. However, there's no denying that the fact he didn't like being called Danny played a large part in the whole sorry scenario.

Arthur had insisted on calling him Danny even though I have no doubt that he knew Daniel didn't like it. Why else would he tell Lucy to be careful to always call him Daniel? For Arthur, the use of the name Danny was a sign of his power over the younger man, a bit like that handshake.

He tried to do that to me earlier but I was prepared for it thanks to what Daniel had told me. Anyway, I used to box for the county when I was young and I still help out at the gym when I get the chance. I'm in pretty good nick for a bloke my age and Arthur Braithwaite hadn't banked on that. My handshake had been more than a match for his.

Daniel's handshake hadn't been though and Arthur used it to exert power over him.

This was all about power. The power that William Morris wanted, the power that Arthur and Lucy had, and the power that Daniel craved.

'It's always about power,' Frank had told me on my first day, 'power or control. Remember that and you won't go far wrong.'

It's advice that has served me well over the years.

Lucy was right when she said that he could have told her that he was married, even though we all know that it wouldn't have made any difference to her. She'd shown no shame when she admitted that. However, she's right when she says that he could have told her. He says he tried to tell her but I doubt he really did. He has tried to say that he was powerless to resist Lucy's charms but that's rubbish. He wasn't powerless, he was just gutless.

I've got to say that I do feel a bit sorry for Daniel because although they have denied it, both of the Braithwaites had a part to play in yesterday's events. I'm not saying that they meant for Isobel to get stabbed but they were the ones responsible for the position that Daniel found himself in. Without them in his life I don't imagine that he would have ever been in that situation. I looked at Daniel's eyes as he was talking about his wife and I think he really does care for her. It's just a shame for both their sakes that that wasn't enough for him. I suspect it would have been had it not been for the intervention of the Braithwaites. The sad truth is that regardless of what I think they didn't actually do anything wrong, not in terms of this incident anyway, so Daniel will be on his own with this one. They may have put him in the situation but he was the one with the knife in his hand.

He says that he didn't realise that he was holding the knife until he saw the blood on his hands but I don't think that will save him if he goes up before a jury.

He wants to count himself very lucky because according to the doctor that I spoke to, if the knife had gone in a couple of inches to the left it would have hit the abdominal aorta and she would have bled to death in less than ten minutes. He'd have been facing a murder charge and the drop then, regardless of whether he knew he was holding the knife or not. As it is, the worst it can be is attempted murder.

I need to speak to Isobel Laither because until we have her version of events we don't know where we're going with this. I rang the hospital this morning before I spoke to her husband and the nurse said that she'd had a comfortable night. She said that if everything was alright when the doctor did his rounds I should be able to speak to Mrs Laither this afternoon.

I wonder if Daniel realises that his future is in her hands.

ISOBEL

Thank you for coming to see me Inspector Deardon. The doctors say I should be able to go home tomorrow but I wanted to see you as soon as possible so that we can get this mess cleared up. I understand you want me to tell you about what's been going on with Daniel.

Well, the first thing I should tell you is that my husband is an uncomplicated man. Some might call him simple and they wouldn't be wrong. He likes the simple things in life and it doesn't take much to make him happy.

His favourite dinner is liver and onions so that should tell you everything that you need to know.

And that's why this is so unexpected; it's just not like him. Having said that, he is a man so I shouldn't have been too surprised. Sorry, I don't mean to be rude but my mother always said that there isn't a man walking the earth that you could trust when it came to this sort of thing.

I thought that Daniel was the man to prove her wrong, and God forgive me I'm glad she's no longer with us because I would have hated to admit to her that she was right.

Daniel and I have been married for over fifteen years and I thought that we were happy. No, more than that, I *knew* that we were happy and we would have stayed that way if that girl hadn't appeared on the scene.

Until this I'd always thought that Daniel was a clever man. He's done very well for himself at the bank and got his own branch a couple of years ago. Stupid men don't get that sort of job. Daniel isn't stupid, which is why I can't understand why he ever thought that girl was actually interested in him.

I've only seen photographs of her in the newspaper but even they show how beautiful she is with her blonde hair and her perfect figure. She could have any man that she wanted, so why would she want Daniel? He says that they are in love but I don't believe that. He says that they are having a baby together... but I don't believe that either.

Come on Inspector Deardon, you're the detective here. Why would Lucy Braithwaite have Daniel's baby? Why would she have anyone's baby? She just wouldn't. It wouldn't fit in with her lifestyle.

I wouldn't be surprised if, when you speak to her, she'll tell you that there never was a baby. I suspect she wanted to see how far she could push him. You've already spoken to her haven't you and she's already told you that there's no baby. I can see it in your eyes.

Maybe I should have shared my theory with Daniel yesterday then I wouldn't have found myself here getting stitches in my side.

I knew about her you know, his other woman, though I didn't know who she was or that she was half his age.

I first started to think that there was a problem towards the end of last year. Daniel started to have trouble sleeping so I knew that something must be wrong. He never has trouble sleeping – he even slept through the air raid siren once. You should have seen the job I had waking him up so that we could go to the shelter.

I don't know if he's told you, but Daniel didn't go to war. He has a medical thing that meant that they wouldn't have him. He's never really talked about it but I think that it made him feel less of a man. From my point of view I was just happy to have him at home with me.

Sorry, you'll have to forgive me Inspector but I've never been interviewed by the police before and I'm a bit nervous. I know that your time must be precious so I'll try and keep to the point from now on.

Like I said, I knew that there was something wrong late last year when Daniel was having trouble sleeping. I asked him if everything was alright and he said that it was but I had my doubts. It all comes back to those sleepless nights.

You see, I'm a bit of an insomniac myself and I haven't had a full night's sleep since about 1937. I've spent many a night lying on my side listening to the sound that Daniel makes as he sleeps. Now, night after night, I was listening to the sound of Daniel awake.

Something was wrong, I just didn't know what.

A few weeks before that he'd told me about a new client that he'd brought to the bank. Obviously he didn't tell me anything that would identify the client but he did say that he was important and that it could mean good things for us. He seemed to think that it might put him in line for a promotion which would be marvellous. We've wanted one of those houses on Chestnut Avenue for a while, so maybe this would be our chance of making our dream come true. He seemed very excited about the prospect. I thought that work might have been the problem.

My guess is that *her* father was the important client and that's how he met her so in a way I was right.

Anyway, we had a lovely Christmas which we spent with our friends Sylvia and Stephen. They both commented that he seemed distracted and I told them that he was under pressure at work. I don't think that they believed me but they were both too polite to say anything.

It was some time in January when I started to think that it was probably a woman that was causing Daniel to lose sleep.

It was a midweek night and Daniel initiated love-making. I know you probably don't think there's anything strange about that because we are married, but I think I could count on the fingers of one hand the number of times that we have made love on anything other than a Sunday night. So that struck me as odd but what Daniel did was even odder.

I think that he realised what he had done because he stopped himself from doing it as quickly as he had started. The thing is, he didn't stop soon enough.

I'm a little embarrassed to tell you that he stuck the tip of his tongue in my mouth and I have to say that I didn't like it at all. I never have and he knows that.

That was when I knew that there was another woman in Daniel's life. One that let him do that sort of thing.

I didn't mention what he had done and maybe Daniel thought that I hadn't noticed. The truth is that if I'd asked him he might have told me and I didn't want to know that I was right. I wanted to be wrong.

Sadly for me, my fears were confirmed in February. Mrs Booth, the vicar's wife, was organising a jumble sale and she asked if anyone had anything that they could donate. The church organ gave up the ghost before Christmas and hymns just aren't the same when everyone is singing to a different tune. One of the parishioners can fix it but we needed to raise the money for the parts. So Mrs Booth organised a jumble sale.

I went through my wardrobe and came up with a few bits and bobs and then I turned my attention to Daniel's things. I knew that he had some shirts that hadn't seen the light of day for a long time so he wouldn't miss them. As I was taking them out of the wardrobe I noticed his old overcoat hanging at the back. I took it off its hanger and as I was giving it the once over I noticed a bulge in one of the pockets. Maybe I shouldn't have but curiosity got the better of me and I had a look at what it was. Part of me was hoping that it would be something pretty like a nice pair of earrings that he'd bought as a surprise for me. I mean, it wasn't my birthday or anything but... well... I was just hoping.

I was disappointed.

I'm sure that you've already heard about the watch.

I sat on the bed for a long time crying and holding the watch in my hands, trying to work out what it meant.

Despite what you might think, Inspector, I'm not a stupid woman and I knew that there was only one reason that my husband was hiding something as beautiful as that watch. He didn't want me to know that he had it, which meant that someone he didn't want me to know about had given it to him.

The Gentleman's Club that he had suddenly started to go to on Thursday nights made sense. Gentleman's Club be damned, he was seeing his mistress on Thursday nights.

I wondered what sort of woman could afford to buy the sort of watch that Daniel kept hidden in the back of his wardrobe, and I imagined her to be a rich widow.

How wrong could I have been?

I put the watch and the coat back where I had found them.

I suppose you think that I was burying my head in the sand. First of all I didn't mention the tongue and then I didn't mention the watch. I've asked myself that question a thousand times and it's always come down to the same thing.

I don't know if you're married Inspector, but to me my marriage vows were sacred. I said the words 'for better or worse' and I also said 'until death us do part.' I made those vows before our friends and before God and I meant to keep them. I meant them then and I still mean them now so no matter what Daniel was up to he was still my husband, and he will remain so until one of us dies. That being the case, it would be easier for me if I didn't know the truth.

Maybe you have to be a woman to understand. Without our husbands, we are nothing.

Around about Easter time Daniel said the he had to go away for work, something about a meeting at Head Office. He said that it involved an overnight stay which I thought was very unlikely but I went along with him.

There was a bit of confusion about how he was going to get there so I suggested he go on the train. You should have seen the colour drain from his face when I said that I would come and see him off at the station. It would have been funny if it hadn't been so serious. The next thing I knew he had come up with a colleague who had suddenly been called to the same meeting. A colleague with a car – wasn't that lucky?

After he left that morning I went to our bedroom and checked in the pocket of his old overcoat.

The watch had gone.

I was almost sick the following day when he came home. All I could smell was her perfume on him. He tried to say that it was someone's cologne but it was like no cologne that I've ever smelled. The thought of them together was almost more than my stomach could stand but I made an excuse about making tea and disappeared off into the kitchen. I went straight to the back door and took in large gulps of air.

I'm not going to pretend that any of this has been easy because it hasn't and you know that I'd be lying if I said anything different. I had to pretend to be the contended wife when, in reality, I was feeling anything but. I had to cook for him, I had to clean for him, and every now and then I had to make love to him.

That was the worst part. The others I could do by rote but when we made love I would torture myself by imagining him with her. He never did that tongue thing again but I imagined that they did it all the time.

I thought that if I waited long enough, whatever he had with whoever she was would fizzle out and he would be my Daniel again.

I thought things might be over between them a few weeks ago when he came home covered in cuts and bruises. He tried to tell me that he'd been mugged but he wouldn't let me call the police. You'd report a mugging to the police, wouldn't you? I thought that whoever she was wasn't a widow after all, she was a wife. I thought that her husband had found out about their carry on and had beaten Daniel to a pulp. I'm a little bit ashamed to tell you that I was quite pleased... not pleased that Daniel was hurt, obviously... but pleased that it was over.

Except it wasn't over. Apart from the day after the beating he continued to go out on Thursday evenings and he continued to come home smelling of her.

My world really started to fall apart last week though when I saw Sylvia in town. She told me about something that Stephen had told her. Apparently Daniel had asked Stephen about how easy it would be to get a divorce. He'd said it was for a friend, but I couldn't help wondering. I think Sylvia must have been thinking the same which is why she mentioned it to me. I tried to tell myself that he really had been asking for someone else, Johnson maybe, but if I'm honest I think I really knew that he was asking for himself.

Which is why I wasn't totally unprepared for what happened yesterday.

Daniel came home as usual but I could tell from his face that there was something wrong. He looked terrible, grey almost. He said that he needed to talk to me.

We were in the kitchen when he said that he wanted a divorce.

I felt like I had been punched in the stomach.

I can't remember exactly what I said but I'm sure that I said 'no.'

Everything is a bit of a blur but that was when he told me that his mistress was no other that Lucy Braithwaite, the socialite daughter of Arthur Braithwaite. He said that he wanted to marry her. He said that she was pregnant.

I sort of snapped when he said that. I'm sure that you already know that Daniel and I have never had children, and the fact that he had given another woman the one thing that I wanted more than anything else in the world was more than I could take.

I'm not proud of the way that I behaved; I was screaming and shouting at the top of my lungs. Goodness knows what the neighbours must have thought.

I didn't realise that the knife was in my side until Daniel screamed.

It wasn't deliberate Inspector, I'm sure of that. Why would Danny want to stab me?

Oh, what happened there? I called him Danny. I think I like the way that that sounds.

Danny.

Danny Laither. I am Mrs Danny Laither.

She's not going to want to marry him now. I'm willing to bet that she never wanted to marry him. I'm sorry, but he's not much of a catch for the likes of her.

He's going to need me now.

Has he told you how much he hates being called Danny? Well you'd better get used to it... Danny Boy.

ACKNOWLEDGEMENTS

This book could not have been written without the support of my family and I need to thank them for that. A particular mention must go to my husband and sons for their love and encouragement. I don't think they understand why I write but they accept that it is part of who I am. I also want to thank my parents and siblings for always making me feel special and for giving me a golden childhood.

As always, I have to give special thanks to the staff of Sunderland Royal Hospital, especially those in ICCU, the renal unit and ward B28. Without their skill I wouldn't be here so everything that I do is a tribute to them.

I would also like to thank my dear friend Jan Weiss. She has been with me since the start of my writing journey and is the only one who truly knows what this means to me. One day I'm going to write a story based on our long-distance friendship that has lasted over four decades.